Harry and the Madman

A Mayhem & Murder Mystery

featuring Harry Saybrook

By

Stephen Dahl

In the Roaring Twenties, many people knew
Philo Vance, pride of Harvard College. Here's a new
private detective, Harry Trumbull Saybrook, a
graduate of Yale, in splendid apposition.

This is a work of fiction and any resemblance to persons
living or dead is coincidental.

1

The driver of the huge Cadillac knew something was wrong, and that an accident would occur. Despite the bright day and the warm breeze, he did not see the motion on the road, and he could not hear the dog's loud barking. It wasn't a real dog, long of leg and ready for the hunt, it was an enormous bag of fluff and curls glistening with diamonds pasted on its collar and small vest.

The animal had rushed out into the street, and jumped up and down ferociously. Perhaps the dog did not like the shiny dark bronze of his auto, the Man started to think, but there was no time. He felt a sudden thump and slowed his vehicle down. In his right rear view mirror he could see the beast squirm and move spasmodically, with surprising energy.

Then, he heard someone scream. Disregarding this plaintive cry, he stopped the Cadillac and reversed it carefully, so that he ran directly over the dog. Then he shifted to DRIVE, went forward, and heard, with

To my long-suffering large-heart

brother

MARK WALDEMAR DAH

With a tip 'o' the hat to Trebor Snede

…and thanks to

Rock Brynner and Christian Angermann

increased satisfaction, another crunch, preceded by a painful yelp. The Man pulled over and laughed to himself.

He had nearly escaped this drama when he heard a series of loud drumbeats on the lid of his trunk. He stopped his car and put the gearshift to PARK. An hysterical woman, seventy-something, changed her pounding from the trunk lid to the windows and came face to face with him, and beat on his window-glass, which he lowered.

"You...*killed my Fee-fee*! You killed *my Fee-fee!*"

He tried to face her directly, eye-to-eye, but her rage was too much, her eyes were bloated with hate, and her artificial eyelashes moved faster than his window-wipers, although, he considered, those had a variable speed control. She finally stopped her screaming and her motions, and sagged momentarily into a shapeless pose, like an effigy ready to be burnt. She wore an assembly of sparkling stones not unlike the canine's, in profusion around her neck, and some on her left wrist, in a resplendent bracelet.

Now her breathing had come back to normal, he looked her in the eye again and said, in his cool whispery voice, "Terribly sorry about that. But the dog ran out in front of my car."

Her heaving breaths showed she was preparing another series of shouts, but, having grown bored with the incident, the Man rolled up his window and returned the transmission to REVERSE. Before she could raise her fists another time, he backed up quickly, about twenty feet. Then, he put it in gear and drove forward, accelerating until the left bumper struck her down. She lay there, a turtle on its back, as he reversed and repeated the tactic.

There was a loud crunching of her arms and thorax as he ran over them, and, again, backing up and gunning the engine, he heard a crackling snap as her head was squashed flat against the pavement. She did not move after that.

Nonetheless, he was enjoying the tactic, and repeated it. The tires ran over the woman's stomach and hips, and left the two bodies erratically stretched, splayed out as if they had tumbled onto hard earth from the stratosphere.

He was now a murderer!

The quiet but lavishly appointed back avenue offered only one witness to the crime, a blue jay, that, on a branch, sat watching. As he drove away the Man reached for a cigarette, which he loved to light with the quick and perfectly balanced coil of orange nichrome — a 'cigar lighter'— that ignited cigarettes with a quiet grace. He rarely smoked. In the rear view mirror he could see the murderous sculpture on the road, but, he inhaled the cigarette and drove off.

He had read about murder and mayhem for years, now he was going to master these arcane arts! His heartbeat ushered him into a new world of action he had many times considered. His hands shook on the wheel. Then he clung to it, hyperventilating. He was Death's minion, he was a sacred Slave, he had tasted the Apple of Eden!

Another look in the rear view mirror showed little of the accident, but he must keep driving. He wished for another backward glance, and wanted to return, but saw a street sign come up which made him smile. "Dog Day Circle", and he knew *that* was the short cut to the golf course.

And, needless to say, *that* is where he went.

2

Harry Trumbull Saybrook was also *en route* to the links. He was, however, lost on another of the shady streets which encompassed the golf club. These roads interconnected, he observed, but rarely offered egress. The development of posh homes was built around a magnificent eighteen hole course that awaited its first PGA tournament, upcoming, it was rumored, though the course had not 'settled' and many of the trees were still saplings. In the Florida climate they would grow quickly, but to no great height — the soil was too sandy for high-flying oaks.

The palms were happy to see him, though, and waved, which he received gratefully, the top down on his turbo-charged Mercedes. He had gotten the convertible in a swap for his 'classic' Corvette. The German car was better made, more roadable, and made that unique percussive 'thunk' when one shut a door. The trunk had a special berth for his golf-bag, and his only expense had been five hundred dollars : pneumatic lifts for the canvas top. He had a hard top for wintertime that screwed on and which he hoped never to use.

There had been a series of dainty red arrows directing him to the clubhouse, but he had lost track of these and, as he looked ahead, he espied, then realized, the horrible tangle of flesh on the road. At first, Harry wondered if it were some Halloween manikin laid out as a joke, until, coming close, he saw the corpses in their bloody disarray.

Briefly, he wanted to vomit, and in the next moment, he wanted to laugh at this grotesque 'modern' art. The dog wore a halo of flies, but the woman's cadaver was pristine. Her jewels sparkled with triumphant brilliance, though her jaw was crushed and open, showing dentures come loose. He could see faint tire tracks of blood, and that the killer had repeatedly run her, and her pet, over and over. Was this someone's murderous revenge or a senseless experiment?

Damn, damn, another 'involvement'!

However carefully he looked, he touched nothing, and pulled to the side of the road to call the police on his new mobile phone.

"You mean, a dog, *and* a woman, have been run over, like, *next to each other!?*" The dispatcher did not impress Harry as astute or credulous. The line crackled slightly before she said, "OK. Car on the way. Would you please…"

He gave his personals and promised not to leave the scene, but fairly ground his teeth as he imagined his tee time at the golf club might be forfeit. The blue jay jumped to another branch and cocked its head. Harry, an erstwhile birdwatcher, saw this with pleasure.

The neighborhood was not populous, such homeowners, he reasoned, cherishing their privacy. The blue jay cocked its head again and Harry wondered what it was thinking, even what it had seen. It gave a chirrup suggesting, thankfully, there were no vultures overhead.

Harry rolled down his window for a better look. It was horrible. An old lady and a spoiled dog. A satirical situation. A Charles Addams cartoon. This dead woman had doubtless treated the pet better than she would have any lost soul, penniless relative, or wayward drunk. The scene, however uncharitable, now offered a view previously unimagined : a helter-skelter of broken limbs inside a Rorschach pattern of darkening blood.

His eye focused on the glitter of diamonds. Could this mischief have been a failed robbery? Perhaps the killer did not take the jewels because of a time factor, or he thought someone watched, or, if it were pure 'accident', he had a deeper motive, perhaps hatred of the ruined female. An unpaid debt? Or, no motive at all! In other words, a vehicular homicide!

He now took a critical look. It was obvious in the execution of the crime, the dog had been run over first, and then squashed, and then, the woman must have come to save the animal, and the killer, perhaps on a wave of sadistic pleasure, decided to complete his treachery. Remove any witness. To "make sure". Unless he had lured the dog there as a Judas goat. That was improbable.

The blue jay appeared in a flash, darted down, and began to peck at the diamonds, then at the dog's eye. It looked to Harry for permission then turned its beak toward the flesh. Ferociously, the exquisitely-colored bird dug into the eye socket and yanked forth a delicious morsel, flapped its wings, and returned to its perch to feast as the police car pulled up.

"You see this happen?" asked the cop in a thick Boston accent. He was big and well-fed, wore polished black boots, with a Prussian stripe upon his trousers. "Just stay in your 'cah'".

"No," Harry said, handing the policeman his driver's license. "I was trying to find the golf course, got lost, and remembered, from before, this area had a shortcut."

The cop handed the license back. "Not many people know that." Harry noticed the cop, big and pushy, when he looked on the street, turned suddenly pale-faced, and ready to regurgitate his proverbial lunch of coffee and donuts. The cop needed several minutes to recover. He did, and approached Harry.

"Jeezus, I knew that old lady, she used to donate to our retirement fund." The big trooper squatted down and eyed the diamonds, then stood up, took off his cap, and wiped his forehead. "I'll bet you the goddam dog has real diamonds too."

"I'm no gemologist, officer, but they sparkle like the real thing. Rhinestones have a pinkish-purple hue. You're looking at half a million dollars of cold ice, I'll bet." This joke supplanted what he'd almost said, "bet you a dollar to a donut," but Harry refrained.

The cop put on his cap. "Whoever ran over Mrs. Zlotkowski left tire marks…" Interrupted by his radio's noisy alert, he confirmed the crime, and put in a request for 'homicide and forensics' which sounded to Harry like 'ham and eggs'. Harry marveled at his belt of bullets, pouches, holsters, handcuffs and…poison gas?

He resembled a state trooper, but this was a local cop, dressed impeccably, and unused to such random acts of violence. He seemed a "good cop", that is, honest and efficient. The man looked at the tire tracks, and snuck back of Harry's Mercedes to compare them. As Harry had paid $200 for each rare Michelin, he doubted two such treads would coincide.

"They're not your tire tracks, Mr. Saybrook, don't worry." He smiled. "But they are new and expensive tires. My guess, Goodyear top of the line. Used on a lot of American luxury vehicles. But I don't think they're standard equipment. Somebody wanted high performance. They're good in a heavy Florida rainstorm."

"Indeed." Harry knew his tee time was past, but, at this moment, did not want to call the club. They would fit him in, and his friend Judge Rugh would wait, predictably, at the bar. "Officer, although the criminal has left *some* spoor, no one is going to spot blood on the tires, considering how many dusty roads are hereabout."

The word "spoor" stopped the officer's busy hand on the clipboard. He looked at Harry, and raised his eyebrows. "What the hell is 'spoor'?" And then, "Don't I know you?"

Harry clarified the meaning of the word and went on, "If you know Mike Herman."

Now the cop smiled. "That crazy s.o.b. In the DB? Yeah, I know 'im. Wish I didn't. He's too smart to be a cop. Told me he'd studied nuclear physics and also got a head start on DNA profiling, and what the hell is that? I swear, though, that guy Herman could memorize your fingerprints."

Harry hadn't seen Mike for, let's see, two years, when they solved a series of murders which involved a real estate swindle. That's when his classmate at Yale was part of the evidence, a murder victim to a chain saw. Fat Old Chad the 'Baby Rone.' A real estate developer who'd wisely married a rich bitch, in truth, a lovely gal. The case was confused and through a departmental error, Chad's head had been filed away, some thought, in a freezer. But it turned out to be afloat in a huge beaker of formaldehyde. Unwilling, Harry got to see it and wished he had not done so. His friend's eyes remained open and had stared at him without a blink.

Now *that* was shocking, like the roadkill, to see your classmate's head (at least, *that* classmate's head) looking back as if he'd been beheaded by a Turk! Who had insisted he see that?

Mike Herman! *That* piece of work! A homicide detective of the first order, handsome like George Segal, or handsome like Tyrone Power, seeing he had a Jewish father and an Irish mom. He wore a holy medallion and said it was "Saint Isidore." Harry had never seen its image, but had heard it was otherwise, something obscene, taken from the hairy chest of a Mafia assassin Mike had been obliged to shoot dead.

"I'll bet you're another smart ass like Mike," the cop muttered. "It figures. It sure seems this is a homicide, from the evidence. *Anyone* can see that..."

The forensics van approached, followed by another police car, its slim roof-lights flashing but with the siren off. Mike wasn't there and Harry was grateful. He was in no mood to help out, but, fate seemed to have inveigled him into a new monstrous scenario.

The first out was the photographer, a woman with terrible legs who displayed no reaction to the scene. Then another woman in a white jacket and with a doctor's bag, Harry presumed, although it was twice as big. The cops in the other car sat idly, not wishing to play 'backup'. One was youthful, displaying a look of horror when he surveyed the dog, and the other, driving, was beefy, like the first policeman. They called him 'Pete'. Occasionally, he worked the microphone and replaced it — officially— on its bracket.

"You can go now, Mr. Saybrook," the first policeman said. Harry gave him his business card. The cop gave him his. **B. J. Willison**. No pushover, this guy. "Call us if you remember further details." The sun was hot, Harry felt his brow must glisten with sweat. But Officer Willison ignored this 'guilty' trademark. "I'll tell Mike I saw ya."

It had been thirty minutes since Harry happened on the scene. Directions were given to him to find the golf course without getting lost. Harry deduced he'd taken two wrong turns, and that if he'd not been so stubborn a pathfinder, he'd have hit his first shot half an hour ago, missed the mess, and been in a much better frame of mind.

He turned the Mercedes around and found the proper turn, after fiddling the phone to call Judge. His call was answered immediately. "Harry," Judge said, "don't hurry. They've set us another time, it will be an hour. Meet me at the Nineteenth Hole, OK?"

"Will it be only an hour?"

"Yeah, a fancy party came in, one of the club owners, friend to neither you nor I. Big old limo. We would have been bumped anyway."

Harry told him what had just happened. Judge whistled, one of his annoying habits. Judge Rugh would also spit to dislodge an annoyance, he gobbled his food, and frequently belched. Sometimes, after a long cool draft of beer, he would wipe his mouth on his sleeve, sigh, and sonorously burp. Otherwise, as a man and magistrate, he was a paragon.

Harry was driving through the club gate and its huge pineapples carved from alabaster when the phone rang again. It was Mike Herman. He saw the name flash and switched off the phone. Harry Saybrook had enough on his mind and feared the tension would disturb his golf swing and bring back the hook he had trained for months to avoid.

But he'd *have* to call Mike back…*later*.

3

Whoever designed the country club and the golf course had the foresight to make the clubhouse road long and full of winding curves. These often traversed a fairway, or a golf-cart crossing, and the warning signs were nearby but popped up unpredictably. One could not, therefore, drive the highway at any speed, ten miles per hour being rightly posted and necessarily observed. One could be hit by a golf shot or one would stop precipitously when a golf cart jumped out. Usually, these dangerous conveyances contained two women in rapid conversation, as in their game they hit a drive, then drove.

Some curves entered a dark clustering of trees, some bypassed sand traps, until one negotiating them attained the long straight stretch to the pillared plantation manse. There the first tee abutted the extensive patio and its umbrellaed tables, and there the eighteenth hole, in a huge kidney shape, embraced the patio's far reach. The "Nineteenth Hole" was technically a small bar under an awning in sight of the final flag. However lengthy the last green, an occasional long approach shot would surmount the protective fence, hit just below the formal balcony restaurant, fall down to the awning, wherefrom it could roll into someone's tumbler or stein. That happened rarely, but the ball would be lost on a two-stroke penalty, and whoever found that ball in his drink, owned it forevermore, as a lucky talisman.

Harry drove into the well-shaded parking lot and sought a huge shadow to save his leather seats from the scorching sun. Further up, near the clubhouse, a stretch limo had arrogated the cobbled walkway, but it was no great obstacle. Of the few cars on the sandy surface of sea shells, Harry noted two BMWs, one Toyota convertible, a nicely restored Mustang in racing regalia, and, he marvelled, an regally restored Cadillac, immaculate, enormous, with oversized chrome bumpers added front and back. Those bumpers meant it was at least ten years old, and they were magnificent, made to order, as lovely a sculpture as the grille on a Jaguar. Harry thought, that Caddie might have been custom built, newer, with some extra trimmings. In the good old days, an auto a bootlegger would choose.

He looked at the clear blue heavens and decided to leave the Mercedes top down. No one had ever been robbed at the club, and it had security cameras aplenty, they said, at least one in the parking lot. Indeed, the large oaken clock face was said to contain one, the minuscule lens invisible, but a virtual Argus. Ineffective!? Mike Herman later complained the tapes were kept for only a few days, were of poor quality and had cost him a previous arrest, the culprit having parked there late at night to sleep. No security guard would question an auto like a Rolls-Royce or an XKE, no big limousine, nor its sleepers.

He popped open his trunk, took out his golf bag, and hefted it on his right shoulder, equal in breadth to his left. It never seemed to matter which, Harry was ambidextrous and, for that reason, deadly on the tennis court. He'd never tried left-handed golf, but vainly assumed it would be no chore to master.

His clubs clacked. He enjoyed their weight, and the history of the bag itself, given to him by Arnold Palmer, whose name and logo, embossed on the leather, reminded him of the first tournament he had won, an amateur. Arnie, smiling and effusive, handed him the bag and the trophy, tendering his congratulations in that Pennsylvania accent that echoes pure Americana. The eighteen-year-old Harry was exultant, as happy as the next month, when his Letter of Acceptance came from Yale.

He had won by four strokes on a tough course that Arnie had designed and helped to build. Golf was Harry's avenue from obscurity and to it; no one seemed curious about a man playing golf, even with an Arnold Palmer bag. Other golfers kept their eye on him, the future champion.

All's one for that!

He looked up at the sky again. Harry rarely took off his sunglasses. They were another personal luxury, made from the same material used by America's fighter pilots. Some kind of desert sounding name, exotic, he could rarely recall. Alarmingly expensive but worth, he thought, their weight in platinum. If one wanted the best, the price could never be too high. Out of reach, one might say, and one should say, loudly, to the covetous.

He examined the glorious Cadillac but did not hear the Man approach. "Like my car?" The voice was smooth and the question barely whispered.

"Definitely." Harry did not look at him. "Did you have this specially restored? I'm looking at the bumpers and all that extra chrome, quite impressive."

The man, of average height and of pleasant appearance, gave a quick description of how the "body by Fisher" had been re-enforced and the suspension improved. The trunk seemed to have been expanded, as Harry noticed when the fellow fetched out his own golf bag. When he saw Harry looking into the enormous cavity and its luxury carpeting, he smiled and kept the trunk lid open. Harry thanked him, noticed his smirk, excused himself, and walked away. Only then did the Man shut the lid, as if he had wanted to air the trunk out. Harry looked back once and was not surprised to see him wiping the chrome with a fancy colored rag, such as one uses to polish silver. The Man stood proudly now, put the rag into his golf bag, and gloried, Harry thought, at his manly image reflected in the opulent décor.

Judge Rugh was nonplussed as Harry related the adventure. He was half-way through a large beer and, for the first time, hiccoughed to his friend. "'Scuse me, old man, but that reminds me of a sick comic strip of a guy who did 'roadkill art'". Then he burped. After a moment of meditation, he drank deeply, put the heavy glass stein down with a thump as if he were in court. He wiped his mouth on a remarkably hirsute forearm. "Damned insane!"

Harry explained he'd already had a call from Mike Herman. "They don't have much to go on, just some tire tracks, and *I* think they could be too much trouble to trace. Or, to find. The worst kind of clue, because people routinely 'adjust' their tires, for higher performance, stopping ability, and the heavy downpours we have here in F-L-A."

"Mike will tell you, doubtless, in greater detail," said Judge. "Clever bastard, I don't like him, but I'm glad you do." He motioned to the waiter for another beer. Harry signaled for the same.

"Did you see who belongs to that stretch limousine in front?"

"Some fancy people, celebrities, but don't ask me. One striking female, that's all I noticed."

"They have their own way of parking." Harry laughed and took up his drink. "Funny thing, I need this right now. It's already searing and the picture of the homicide is dancing in my head…like sugar plums, *squashed* sugar plums."

His phone rang again, it was Mike. He answered on speaker setting so Judge could hear. "Harry! My faithful sleuth! You would have to arrive on the scene. What do you make of it?"

"Not much. It was obvious, from the tire tracks, that the manslayer deliberately ran down the old gal. Unless some one can concoct a scene where she was targeted, and the dog came running to her assistance. It makes more sense if — let's say — the murderer was waiting to run the dog over so she would come out. She looked to be rich as Midas, covered in diamonds, and I'll wager the dog wore real stones, not something fake."

"The deceased was one Zelda Zlotkowski and she *was* richer than Midas. She'd lived on that patch for twenty years and her husband had helped develop the land. He died five years ago, and she's remained a rich secluded widow. We spoke to the neighbors and they didn't know her for beans. Never came out, not even for mail, which was delivered on her porch."

After a swallow Harry answered, "There are nutters who deliberately cruise for dogs, and anything else they can run over. I guess that excludes deer or foxes, but the latter should be harder to hit than…let's say…cats."

"Try armadillos! Truth be told, I've never seen any wild animals at any hour in that area, but no, there are always racoons, and possums. The latter will stare into your headlights and, before they die, give you a hideous grin. No, it must have been unexpected, she had the kettle on and a teapot full of Earl Grey. The kettle was half full, so your timing must have been spot on."

Harry adjusted his sunglasses. "Well, Mike, I'll spare you the old joke about a hit-and-run pregnant nun counting double. But, man being the most dangerous game, there must be some psycho out there looking to drive his truck into a Twinky-fed housewife. Why did the chicken cross the street? We all know it was to teach the possum how much fun *that* could be."

Stifled laughter. Mike rang off after promising to buy Harry a lite lunch of "kosher corn beef and cabbage." Which made Judge laugh. "That's right, he's half Jewish, half Irish. A product of the Dublin slums."

"Rather, following in the steps of Leopold Bloom. No, Mike is unusual for more reasons than his heritage. He was so bored with Dublin he had to get out. Came to New York and became a cop. Rose quickly, then came here. Covering both bases, methinks."

"Rose who? Rose Quickly. Dame Quickly? Shakespeare? Falstaff?"

"No bibliography needed. I got the pun."

"Sorry, I've done better." Judge looked to the first tee, "No one there. Well, if you're bored with Dublin, and come to New York, it doesn't follow you'd end up in Florida, the most boring place on earth." He pointed. "There's no one there, let's grab the tee."

A few minutes later, they were there, bags in hand. It was almost desolate, and Harry expected that the man in the fancy Cadillac might have been ahead of them. He recounted the brief meeting to Judge. "A strange man, but totally nondescript. I saw his bag of clubs in the trunk, but wanted to catch up with you. But then, I'm too curious when I meet a stranger."

Judge had arranged for the golf cart, as they stood in neat rows nearby. He put his tee in the ground and began to affix the ball. Harry was never surprised to find Judge had the latest and most scientifically advanced brand of golf equipment, even the balls. Harry had stuck with Titleists and had no desire to change. It seemed…unpatriotic.

Judge drove competently and looked proud. "You know, Harry, some people that 'rebuild' cars, they have compartments to smuggle drugs. It's all carefully engineered. During Prohibition, they had an extra gas tank for booze."

"That trunk looked pretty empty to me. It could easily have held ten golf bags."Harry's drive was splendid, and all he needed was a pitching wedge to reach the green. Judge's remark made him think, maybe the strange man could be a drug pusher, he had made a delivery, perhaps to the high rollers in the limousine. No, too much imagination, 'tis enough! The fellow simply changed his mind, or his partner didn't show. The picture of Zelda Zlotkowski on the pavement haunted him. Stop, stop imagining!

They rode together in the cart, more tipsy than they. They hadn't done a round in a year. Friendship from the Good Old Days in New Haven. Boola-boola-boo!

"Time is late, let's just play nine," Judge insisted.
"OK by me, old sport!"

In the parking lot, the wonderfully appointed Cadillac with the magnificent chrome had long since departed.

4

It was impossible to enjoy one's meal when, in this very sporty restaurant, a woman sat smoking and talking in the coarse accent of Pawtucket, Rhode Island. She was lamenting the retirement of her hero, Larry Bird, whom she reiterated as "*Mah Burd*," over and over, in a great exhalations of smoke.

The Man could see she was between fifty and sixty beneath her thick make up, and that her teeth were irregular, to terrify a child or to delight an orthodontist. All her clothing was made of polyester something. She was plain, but no troll, vulgar in mien, and roughly efficient in her assertions. She kept talking, talking. The man who sat at her table was only visible from the back. His jacket was a well-worn Madras, with strained threads near each shoulder, and distinct wear on the elbows.

"Are we going to the track *or not?*" she demanded.

Her companion shrugged, and answered, in a similar Rhode Island drawl, "Don't think so. Too hot today." When she took out another cigarette, he lit it. She heaved another huge breath of nicotine, and put her elbows on their table.

"I thought we were going to the track."

Her friend straightened his jacket and shook his head. "I thought so too, but didn't bring much cash."

"At the track they got one of those ATMs you can get cash from!"

That fellow's torpor was enviable, the Man thought. How could he put up with that woman, no, they weren't... married? No. Husbands don't light their wives' cigarettes, do they? He imagined the endless vapid conversation the other chap must endure. They were brother and sister, *that* seemed, from appearances, to be plausible. Then the woman inhaled and looked at the wall adjacent. It was a sports bar, and there, obviously, would be a picture of Larry Bird.

There was. Even an old black and white of Bob Cousy, and numerous Celtic stars, against a background of shamrocks affixed to wires so they moved occasionally, as if in a meadow. A small leprechaun in plastic tipped his hat up to this heroes' gallery. The woman sighed, loudly as before, *"Mah Burd!!!"*

"If there was a local basketball team I'd take you there," her table mate said. "But there ain't. We could see a movie."

At his table, watching the lethargic drama, the moderate medium mystery Man finished his fish and chips. This bar served the best. Something made him very angry, at first he thought, it might be the oil they cook it in. Liverish? No, he was irritated by the atmosphere of smoke and mirrors, and the sports bar, more a mausoleum than a hall of fame. It obviously attracted a northern clientele, Bostonians and Rhode Islanders. The big cop who just left also spoke to the barkeep in the New England brogue. When he looked up again, he saw the man in the colorful jacket walking out, but the woman remained. She tapped her fingers on the table, and he noticed her eyes were almost Asiatic, hooded and beady. Her lipstick was uneven, and her ashtray was full. She focused on the sporting portraits again and sighed. The

Man said to himself, "If you say 'my Bird' again, I'm going to kill you."

Then he thought, *"I am going to kill you!"*

She mouthed the words, he was sure, but no sound ensued. The Man felt his revulsion rising, rising. The woman sat in a reverie with her cigarette and its dwindling fumes. She frowned and shook her head. He saw her take a ring of keys from her purse, and find the ignition key, which bore a cloisonné emblem. She smiled proudly and got up. Having looked at the wall one last time and then, hesitatingly, at the door marked LADIES she paused, but turned away and made for the exit to the parking lot.

Of course, he followed.

5

The Man wondered at first if the blowsy lover of Larry Bird, who smoked like a chimney, would notice the huge Cadillac that pursued and catch the glint of its magnificent chrome. Her rear view mirror was, however, aligned for putting on lipstick at the first stop light. She'd headed for the main drag but bypassed the big shopping mall for a standalone store, ONE DOLLAR. They were sprouting up all over the state, but he'd never tried shopping in one, *if* one could "shop". He imagined bins of junk from liquidators, but had been told the displays were neat and most discounts applied to smaller sizes of brand name goods.

This outlet featured a massive Christmas sale, though it was not quite Halloween. Before exiting her auto, some kind of Plymouth, the woman had neatened her coiffeur and readjusted her rear view mirror. She removed her seatbelt carefully and he saw she counted cash out and folded it up and, he guessed, tucked it away in her brassiere. He'd not noticed her figure but she was bosomy and wide hipped, with barely passable legs. She wore no socks and her shoes were cheap fringed moccasins.

He wanted to retch when he recalled her smoky idolizing of Larry Bird. For no reason, it had poisoned his outlook. Perhaps they had posters of Larry Bird in the store, or portraits of "*mah Burd*" done on black velvet, next to those of Elvis. He made out an odorizer hanging from the rear view mirror shaped into the Celtics' leprechaun. Otherwise, her car was plain but shiny, and this being Florida, there was no safety sticker, just a mildly faded license plate of standard issue.

Once, he had a marvellous pair of Nikon binoculars for surveillance, now, it was a pen-sized Zeiss monocular he could use without being noticed, covering it as if he blew his nose. That allowed him to scrutinize, across the street, the hoop earrings of coral hue which stayed in place as she bounced into the emporium. He replaced it inside his jacket when she finally emerged, bustling and carrying two large yellow plastic bags. *Got those bargains!* From one protruded a large styrofoam candy cane. She put the bags next to her, and nodded her head, as if she had done a great deed, then started the car and drove decisively away.

He pulled out to follow her, but a police car cut him off, its siren and lights going, apparently off to another emergency, a fender bender or some motorist with a flat. So, he almost lost her, but caught sight of the Plymouth at a red light down the road. She was reviewing her make up in the rear view mirror, and, if she did recognize him, it didn't matter.

She drove the back streets very fast, half-running most STOP signs, and went down a dusty lane to her house, a small bungalow near the street's end. It was unremarkable, but an American flag fluttered from a pole centered in the front yard, surrounded by a circular bed of flowers, petunias, he thought, not knowing much about gardens. A woman like that would love "petunias."As he pulled his car to a stop he reached inside his vest to remove the automatic pistol. Deftly he took out the silencer and forced it in place. Then, letting his hand drop down, he got out.

"Doing some shopping?"

She had not fully exited the Plymouth, trying to balance her legs while holding the two bags of Christmas decorations.

She looked at him angrily, as if he'd tried to peer up her skirt, then anchored her feet on the ground.

"*Who are you?*" She fussed with the bags and he could see a Santa Claus outfit inside one.

"I'm the president of the local Larry Bird Fan Club," he replied. She started to smile, then turned wary. But she looked puzzled, not scared.

"I didn't know there was one," was all she could say before he interrupted, "This is from Larry Bird."

She was more confused when he raised the automatic and shot her between the eyes. Her jaw moved up and down a few times, then she fell back into the car, her head askew and her mouth open wide, the tongue protruding in the way taxidermists display tongues when they mount a wild bear or a wild boar.

The supercharged hollow point bullet had gone into her cortex and exploded, for her eyes now bulged much like a frog's. It was a perfect shot, the entry wound near invisible. The Man thought idly, "she's seen a ghost" but, no, she had seen *him*. He laughed softly. Somewhere in her dying brain was *his* image. He thought of that later with hypocritical nostalgia when he relished the perfection of his attack.

Put the gun away first.

He reached into the Christmas bag and took out the styrofoam candy cane and a Santa Claus hat. Then he tipped her face forward and put the hat on, pulling it down past her nose. It was easy to arrange her arms so she gripped the candy cane. Something was wrong: her legs stuck out and the car was open. So, carefully, he lifted the right leg into position, then the left, and shut the door.

"Larry Bird is going to miss you," he said in his usual tone, quiet yet now with the sonority of a benediction. He picked up the brass casing, not that it mattered, a mere .25, perhaps it should be left to confuse the cops.

No. Throw it away later.

One hundred yards off, there was boy riding his bike and coming this way. So, he got into his car and retraced his route. As he approached the kid he rolled down his window, slowed the car, and said, "Hi there! Did you know that Santa Claus is coming to town?"

The kid stopped his bike and, delighted, moved his close-cropped head up and down. The Man rolled up his window and drove smoothly off. Later on, he tossed the casing out, where it flew on the slipstream into a meadow of daisies. The silencer had worked so well, his first thought had been the pistol misfired. No, he'd built it according to a simple blueprint. After all, it was a five hundred dollar fine in Florida even to possess one!

Keeping his eyes on the road now, he fairly growled. The law was grossly unfair to gun enthusiasts! But it had been clever to salute the kid, because the kid would remember him and not his ostentatious automobile. Hated to admit it, but his face was plain and easily forgotten. He hoped.

This anonymity was erased ofttimes by a devilish smile.

6

Mike Herman's desk was an ongoing work of disorganization : pencils, notes, ball points, two staplers, a defective Rolodex, and a .38 cartridge that had no bullet, but which shot up into a flare. "Just in case I get lost in the Everglades." There was a neat center area on the desk top, like a golf course green, in fact, the blotter was made of a green material that, covered with scribbles, looked also like a wall of graffiti, and contained more unlisted phone numbers than Errol Flynn's vanished black book.

Mike was now confronted with a new homicide, by auto, deliberate as one from the muzzle of a gun, or the thrust of a knife. The photos said much, proved Harry's point, or, even his patrolman's assertion, that Zelda Zlotkowski had been deliberately killed. The strange twist, that the murderer could have staged the incident with the dog, to remove motive, jangled his mind. He could neither accept nor reject the premise. Instinct dictated he would need Harry on this case, no one else shed that piercing tunnel of light or made the investigation so much fun.

There was only one heir, a daughter who lived in Los Angeles, plus grants to various charities, none of which needed to hire a hit man to stay in business. He had one case like that previously. A church minister killed his richest parishioner for life insurance. Money, money, the desire of which caused so many, many deaths! Or, in innocence, adorned a small French poodle with a ten thousand dollar diamond collar!

Zelda had been steamrollered by a heavy car with wide tires, and, per his intuition, they were commonly available and several hundred, he knew, had been sold in the last year within his jurisdiction. Which meant little, the driver could be from anywhere. Forensics thought it could not be a truck or SUV, it was a big car, a Cadillac, a Lincoln, an Oldsmobile, a Buick, a Bentley or Rolls-Royce. All these could wear the tires indicated, but so could many trucks. The wheelbase estimate determined it to be a luxury vehicle, not a truck, but the measurement was imprecise.

He tapped his desk with the singular ball-point Harry had given him, he knew that huge autos like that were plentiful in this area. The pen was unique, it contained a small recorder that could capture two minutes of good audio. It took a Cross cartridge and wrote perfectly. No one but he and Harry knew its secret function. Something obtained from a friend of Harry's in the CIA, good old "Roger."

"Now if it was an accident, it must be pure chance…the dog ran out…was hit…then followed its owner…".

His secretary, Hillary Petton, put down a fresh coffee. "You're talking to yourself again, Mr. Herman."

"Oh, thanks. Guess so. Tell me when I begin to answer myself, OK?"

"Mr. Saybrook left a message about dinner at the Golf Club, for five p.m." She stood in place, an immovable Caryatid. "I accepted for you."

"Thanks and thanks again, Miss Petton…"

She bristled slightly. "That's *Ms* Petton, *Mister* Herman." And tapped him on the shoulder.

Mike was sick of female politics, pro or con. It seemed more women than ever wanted to argue with you, show you how smart they were, smarter than you, but remained altogether complacent, with a conciliatory "I love you."

He drained the coffee in several gulps, swallowed hard and returned her gaze. "Is that a hit…or a Mizz?" He received a harder push on his other shoulder as Hillary took the cup and left. He shook his head and said to himself, "if this be flirtation, make the most of it."

The Golf Club was a sports bar offering an excellent grille. Over its entryway was a huge driver, dulled by the sun, but at night there were neon lights that went from driver, to iron, to putter, and then a golf ball which spun and disappeared. Harry sat at the back, nurturing a Campari with soda and lime. Above his right shoulder was a portrait of Bobby Jones, who, truth be told, was one of his ten heroes. Many athletes were admirable, few heroic. He also liked Jim Thorpe.

Harry Saybrook, as an athlete, performed well at both tennis and golf, but kept "in shape" by swimming laps in his own pool. His cozy home was a walk of the Atlantic. He could be lulled to sleep, therefore, by the waves and their lush splashing chorus. The lullaby of night was continued by numberless crickets and frogs, and the morning sea-air — better than a cigarette, though he had quit those two years ago in celebration of his divorce from Louisa Davenport French. One couldn't "drink to that."

"Is this your treat?" Mike asked.

"When has it not been?" Harry answered always refusing to take Mike's crinkled dollars. The detective often wanted to go to another sports bar, the B-Ballers, which Harry rejected as "fit only for the illiterate", and Mike replied, "That's why I like it".

The Irish side of Mike liked that pub because of its atmosphere (very smoky) and its supply of dark beers (Guinness et. al.) and its abundance of low-lifers. Mike

Herman could play the charming Irishman there and survey the burgeoning criminal classes. His particular genius was that the under-worldlings never knew he wore a badge but listened to their shop talk.

The Golf Club's gastronomic peculiarities, such as fritters shaped like golf balls, even with dimples, were hot, tasty and served with seafood and chicken. Harry had ordered a basket of such and they both ate with gusto. "Mine has corn," he said, showing its interior, and Mike replied, "To be expected."

"It's to their credit they fry these things with almost no grease," but Mike pointed to the napkin in which they came and its shiny saturation. "Better there than here," he said, biting into another. After three or four, and a plank of chicken, one had no further appetite, they were that good. The restaurant, realizing that, had upped the price regularly, but also, the substance of the serving. "Now there's a golf ball for you, Mike. If only this place promoted tennis."

"Let me ruin your appetite with some paltry facts about our dead Mrs. Zlotkowski. She's lily-white, no record, no reports, no home invasions…nothing. She loved her dog more than anyone and there is only a far-away daughter, in Los Angeles. Her neighbors say she had few visitors, but they hardly kept watch. The house had up-to-date alarms, but as the killer left twenty thousand worth of diamonds on the road, that is irrelevant. The coroner was shocked by how many broken bones there were; the crushing of her head was something of a *coup de grâce*." He took up one last morsel. "Have you ever run over a turtle? Gives the same thrill, I guess."

Harry found his delight in the crunchy fritter diminished. He finished his drink. He was no longer hungry, not from disgust, but he was ravenous for more knowledge about the crime. The dearth of detail sent a shiver through his guts, from the utter horror of the mayhem also, yet, they had nothing to go on. As Mike chatted he was unsurprised to find the tire tracks inconclusive and that the mad driver had not left his car. That said something. There were no footprints, no other clues, or they had faded fast.

"Murder by automobile," Mike added, "or as we say, a 'vehicular homicide'. Any good lawyer could get the guy off with such a plea. Manslaughter, I mean. Even with that salient malice."

"Need it be a man?"

Mike nodded. "Statistically men are more cruel, unless it's a woman avenging herself. That guy ran over Zelda four or five times, and the dog more than once. Hardly a charitable nature."

"No other similar cases?"

Mike shook his head emphatically. "It's truly rare. You can have a drunk driver run over three or four schoolchildren at a stop, it happens, that's reprehensible. In one fell swoop. Not too many dogs in this area get run over, they're not allowed to roam, kept inside. This bitch, FiFi, the mutt's name, old man, did get out. The garden latch was undone. We haven't caught up with the gardener yet, but I think that will be another profitless link in this greasy chain of accident."

"Still, it rankles," Harry said. "I'll put twenty on its reoccurrence within sixty days. The murder of an aging dame, that is."

Mike's phone lit up and he answered. He said nothing but the pain on his face said 'bad news.' "Almost, Harry, but no bet. There's been another murder, another late-middle-aged single lady, but this one is by gunshot. I'm told there are similar tire tracks, but, let's not jump to conclusions. We might get lucky on this one, at least it took place in a somewhat populous neighborhood where someone *might* have seen it. There *have* to be footprints or fingerprints. The killer left his victim in her car. One shot between the eyes, almost no blood, no mess. They think she's been dead less than two hours."

"That separates the crimes by maximum of five hours," Harry offered. "If it's the same man, he's going on a spree. Your first serial killer!"

Mike laughed and finished his drink. "Serial killer, here's a true story. I'd had a long night and was eating breakfast, my usual Cheerios and milk, and was so hungry I ate too fast, then ordered another.

"The waitress asked me, 'You really like your food, what's your job?' At my wittiest, I said to her 'I'm a cereal killer'. She got scared and called the police. When they came I told them the joke even though they knew me. The waitress still didn't get it. But Willison, that big cop you met earlier today said 'Lady, don't report no body who eats Cheerios'. She *still* didn't get it but I doubt we'll hear from her if a real serial killer stops by."

"You never know, " Harry said. "Be glad it wasn't the 'breakfast of champions.'"

"Want to come along on this one, you might as well. Two can investigate as cheaply as one."

Harry got up with him. "One thing, Mike, you should check on that stretch limo at the club. My intuition smells a strange perfume, can't say why."

"Gotcha, Mr. Ivy League. You gotta biggah nose. But you be right, funny things do add up."

"Spare me the regionalism, what ever it was!"

They left.

7

"It was the UPS guy who found her." Mike stepped carefully toward the auto and opened the Plymouth driver door. *Rigor mortis* had begun, the woman was partially rigid. No one had touched the body, and forensics, already overworked with the hit-and-run fatality, was "on the way."

'Bozo' Willison, smiled to himself when he saw Harry tagging along with Mike. "Youse guys old pals." He knew Harry was smarter than Mike, at least Mike told him that. Mike was a smart-ass also, and Bozo subscribed to the theory that experience equals knowledge, the more you experienced, the more you knew. Smart guys weren't really more intelligent, they could just think quicker. If he leaned close to some high class or high school speedster, with his impenetrable mirror sunglasses inches away, they couldn't think or be smart, they turned chicken-shit and spilled the beans.

After looking inside the car, with a brusque efficiency, Mike told Willison not to worry, just don't leave prints. He'd already put on two latex gloves, and went round the car and opened the passenger door. He gingerly pulled open the yellow plastic bag. Bozo now had his gloves on, twice the size of Mike's.

Harry stood by, hands in his pockets. "Aren't you going to look for a dead dog?"

Mike replied with a frown, then, "This is a different crime. Our victim died instantly, bullet in her brain." He lifted the Santa Claus hat and pointed to the hole in her face. "I'd say, a .25 calibre. Too big for a .22. Exploding point. My gawd, look at those...*eyes*."

Harry averted his gaze, he knew they would be horrible, those 'eyes'. Yet he glanced and was dismayed. He stood back. "Did you find out what the UPS man was delivering?"

"Oh, no, Harry. Check it out. Big flat package over there. Open it, OK? It sure can't have her prints on it."

The package yielded on its label the name of the dead woman and addressee, Beulah Braintree, and inside, a neatly assembled package of basketball posters, two of

Larry Bird. "Ugly cuss, ain't he?"said Harry, and returned the display into its cardboard portfolio.

"Great player! " countered Bozo Willison. "A very great player!" Bozo wanted to take the package home, trophy of battle — no way — it was evidence.

"They'll have to do prints here," Mike said. "Whoever shot good old Beulah left some, I'm sure. Something tells me we won't have them on file. O, mores, O, dactyloscopy!"

"We wax eloquent," Harry said. "But I know what you mean."

"That means fingerprint science," Bozo informed Harry, who flashed back a look of thanks. Willison held up the poster and smiled with admiration, nodding his head.

"That's one approach," Harry answered, turning to Mike. "There has to be some cordite residue, perhaps the powder can tell us…well, about the .25 calibre, if that's what it is. Not many people have that kind of pistol, and, how many manufacturers of such cartridges can there be?" He adjusted his shades. "Just an idea."

"Good point," said Mike. "The scene of the murder is, thankfully, straightforward. The murderer either waited here or followed Beulah home. The latter I like, as she was shopping. Well, maybe not. He could have waited in this area. She might have known him, or he surprised her. I'm sure she didn't get out of her car. Look up the road, there's two houses with windows facing, hopefully a neighbor saw what took place. But it must have happened *so quickly*. The killer might have looked like he was helping Ol' Beulah out of her car, or just stopping by. Bang! She's dead. He arranges the body, he sees the bag full of Christmas stuff, and makes his joke. Time elapsed, two minutes, max."

A call came through on Willison's radio. "Forensics. They'll be here in ten."

"You can go, Boze. Do a neighborhood check in the morning. Or now, I don't care."

"Over here, " Harry shouted. "Car tire tracks but, more importantly, *bicycle tire tracks*."

"Killer on bicycle, then leaves by auto?"

"No, Mike, the bicycle tracks are over the killer's tire markings, which go over Beulah's. That Plymouth tire is narrow, as even Bozo could tell you."

Officer Willison had already left. Another car approached, a Lincoln, but it was not forensics. A man in a Madras jacket got out. "What's going on here?" he asked, as if on one lung. He mopped his forehead with a handkerchief and approached.

"No closer!" Mike said sternly. "This is a crime scene. There's been a murder." He put up his hand to stop the heavy-set visitor. "There would be a ribbon up but we just got here."

"Who got murdered?"

"The lady that lives here. You must know her, you drove right up and stopped. May I see your identification?"

"My gosh, it's Beulah! That's my sister! I'm her brother Bob Braintree. Goddam, how the hell could she get herself shot? She was as dumb as a dumbbell, but didn't have no enemies…"

"How do you know she was shot?" Mike asked.

"Well, I kinda assumed. You said 'murder'. I can see her slumped over in the car, well, I guess she coulda been strangled, but *my* intuition…"

Mike gave the man his card and returned his license. "I'm the homicide detective on this case, Mr. Braintree, and we'll need more than your 'intuition'. The forensics vehicle will be here, but I'd like some answers first. You'll need to come to the station tomorrow as well." He pointed at Bob Braintree, who stood rigid, and wagged his finger. "Speak!"

"Jeez, officer, Beulah and I moved down here from Rhode Island together. Her husband had died and she leant on me for any advice I could give, it wan't much. She liked Florida and found this house and bought it. That turned out good, she kept fixing it up, and if you go inside, you'll see she'd good taste in furniture, and decorations…". He shook his head and began to cry. "Can't I at least see her up close?!"

Mike shook his head and wagged his finger again. Braintree turned angry, but as Mike continued to point at him, and jabbed him several times. Braintree then looked sad, and scared. Taking a breath, he continued, "We thought today might be lucky at the dog track, or that we'd go shopping, that is, Beulah would go shopping, or that we might see a movie, but couldn't make our minds up so we had lunch at the B-Ballers Sports Bar. She likes that because for years Beulah had a crush on Larry Bird, a crazy crush, you couldn't say nothing bad about him. Larry Bird actually came to the B-Ballers to visit after he retired, and when Beulah heard about that she kept going to that place 'cause she hoped he'd come back there another time."

Harry signaled to Mike the forensic van was coming. Mike ignored him and faced Bob Braintree, this time poking him on the worn Madras lapel. "Keep talking!"

"We had lunch there and couldn't agree on what to do. I got impatient and left. Beulah is used to that. She used to have me around her little finger, no more. I went home and had a nap. My neighbor saw me. She'd mentioned something about making me some fancy supper, so here I am. All I remember is that she said something about shopping on the way home."

"Did she say what she wanted to buy?"

"No, never does. She'll be driving along and see a store then just pull over and go in. She likes bargains and mentioned something about doing Christmas shopping early, but it wouldn't surprise me if she went and bought a costume for Halloween!" Mike could see Braintree's fascination with the Santa Claus hat, and patted him on the shoulder.

"OK, Bob, we'll see you tomorrow. Ten a.m. The address is on my card. If you think of anything, call and leave a message. And I mean *anything*".

Before he left, Bob tried various angles to see his dead sister in the car. He seemed not to understand that she had been perversely festooned for the upcoming holiday, ready to meet Santa and to dance with the elves.

The ladies from forensics were disgruntled at having this mayhem double-header. "Mike, we want overtime!" He laughed. "About time you actually worked. Give me a tape." When they handed it to him he put it carefully up on the posts at Beulah Braintree's driveway entrance. He looped one end so one could raise and enter, then replace the barrier.

Harry thought it odd no one else had come to snoop. Certainly others in the neighborhood, sleepy though it was, would be curious. "Let's go," Mike said. "Tomorrow's another day."

The sun was near the horizon, and just before they parted, a ring-ring was heard and the boy on his bicycle rode by. His basket held three rolled newspapers, one of which he tossed onto Beulah's porch.

"Hey, sonny!" Harry shouted. The boy turned around, but Mike said, "He's delivering his newspapers, we'll quiz him tomorrow."

"See you later!" Harry waved.

The boy turned again and pedalled hard. "Hey mister, guess what? Santa Claus is coming to town!"

Mike looked at Harry and muttered, "*Jeezus Christ!*"

Harry adjusted his sunglasses and answered, "How about 'Saint Nick'?"

8

The Man in the huge customized Cadillac felt proud and pleased. He kissed the .25 automatic, a Colt, for its beauty and its dire usefulness. The small pistol was a masterpiece of manufacture and design. It fit his hand and he could conceal it there, or transfer it to a small holster on his belt. There were eight more cartridges inside its clip, and theoretically, eight more people he could murder.

He had been moved by instantaneous disgust to kill the mouthy woman in the sports bar. It had been a happy unhappy happenstance. The Man now admired his own courage. Without hesitation he had followed his quarry, crossed her threshold, and in a strange, gentlemanly way, shot her in the head. The hollow point bullet had exploded perfectly and this ugly female, with repulsive teeth, was dead, with her eyes bulging out like unripe kumquats. That gave him a thrill each time he recollected

it. Execution of the damned, the damned ugly, t..
them into grotesqueries.

Metaphysics told him that all life was kill, or be
killed. Each human was doomed to die, that everyone
admitted, but many believed their deaths would ensue
from a calculus of fate. Their number would come up,
they would die of cancer, or in an airplane crash, or on the
highway in an extravagant collision, or they would feel a
painful seizure in their chest, and stop breathing. Death
had *them* on a *list*. That he, the Man, invisible as Death,
could insert himself into this matrix, satisfied his
predatory soul.

After shooting the loquacious harridan, he had
driven straight home — a condo with a parking garage —
home sweet home, with climate control and numerous
indoor plants. He set the pistol by his bed and flopped
down. Instant sleep, one unforgettable dream: He was an
eagle with claws sharpened on a mountain-top, then the
eagle swooped down, to squeeze and pierce the life out of
vulnerable passersby. The eagle did not devour its prey, it
flew on. The eagle knew there would always be a new

target for its fury in the teeming town. So, famished, it returned to the rocky crag.

When he awoke, it was still night, night filled with city lights, and overhead, Orion with his belt of stars. Orion was the mighty hunter, *he* was Orion, who was once Nimrod, hunter of men. He checked the calendar on his new electronic watch, and determined that he had slept all night, and the entire next day.

Where had the eagle flown, where would it fly next?

These were morning thoughts at midnight. Outside his door was the newspaper, yesterday's, but it contained nothing about the murder of the strange woman with her Christmas bag or the foolish Mistress of the Poodle. Perhaps the police held back the news, and did not wish to reveal details unique to either killing, for fear of a copycat. It occurred to him that the two killings could not possibly be associated: one was an accident, it could be said, the other, most definitely, a cold-blooded homicide. As for the time, he had sandwiched them closely. The boy on the bicycle might possibly identify him, *but*...the youth had pedalled by so blithely, the Man doubted the kid would retain anything but the quirky Christmas wish. Now, if the police interviewed him, what would the boy say? Would he suddenly recall the shining exterior of his car, and all its gleaming chrome?

No, he had left the perfect red herring. If he had seen just the Caddie, it would be valuable evidence, a lead. But the kid would surely make odd puerile commentary, and the flat-footed cops would be fooled.

In the split second after pulling the trigger yesterday, or day before, as it was not quite midnight, the Man realized, time confused, that he was destined to a lifetime of murdering, he was now baptized in fire *and* blood. His nature, a manslayer, a shooter, a simpleton who held the release rope on a guillotine, a hangman's apprentice...it had come with time, time! Time, heartbeat of the universe? Time, the face of the clock? Time, that set the seconds and put a number to events?

He did not care. A new man, with a unique purpose, to outwit all authority and establish his own. He was happy to be Death's acolyte.

The palpable excitement of killing the bitch with the Rhode Island accent, lingo of Pawtucket, or Woonsocket, lived on inside him. That act of mercy, when the pistol fired, that delight he could share with no one, *that* had been slightly extinguished by a sentimental afterthought as he decorated the victim.

I have killed Mrs. Santa Claus!

No more of that silly sadism, so, selfishly, why deny himself *any* dark luxury? He didn't want to conclude that both murders were circumstantial, they had in fact arisen from a chance encounter with detestable patsies, they were ironic sacrifices that someone else should have made, and poured out the blood, *except that he had, circumstantially*, been *there* to do it!

The next target must be chosen, it must be a perfect target, and his next shot must strike its bull's-eye and make a searing black hole, even if no elegant method

came to hand. Method, yes, method to his madness!
Which meant, 'organization.'

He now advised himself, "You must think
categorically, that will work." At his desk he took a pad,
and pigeonholed a few ideas:

1. Prostitute, male or female
2. Pimp
3. Drug addict or dope-head
4. Policeman eating fried chicken
5. Real estate agent of either sex
6. Fat businessman smoking a cigar

He wrote these out carefully with a broad-nibbed
pen and left space for names of people he knew, but the
only one he could fit in was number four, and he thought
of a large local gendarme eating, as always, something
fried. Although he did not know the policeman's name or
badge number, he knew one guy's beat and where he
could be found feeding. However, in his guts he realized,
the last person a budding serial killer should seek should
be a cop. You'd have the whole force on the lookout, and

your career would soon end. Circumstance, like Lady Luck, favored the Men in Blue.

Nor did he wish to select a woman. The first two had been no challenge, but in this resort neighborhood, surely a male prostitute could be found. They were called "chickens" he had been told. "Sir, can I be your chicken?" "Of course, young man. Hop into my Cadillac and we'll drive about in luxury." "Oh, Sir, thank you! I will be a good, good chicken!" "Then, young man, I will not put you in the deep fryer."

But — it would be just as easy — to find a pimp.

He was greatly amused by his strategy, but, before falling asleep again, and that was not easy, the Man confessed he mustn't be too strict on coming categories. Leave room for novelty, leave room for…perfection! But give me patience, I can barely wait! Sweet Murder, stand by my side! Sister of Death!

9

Harry told himself, no matter how close in time and place, the two murders were likely un-connected. One had to be pure chance, the diamond-collared dog dashing out, the hysterical owner, the wanton crushing; the other was a calculated shooting — by a man, undoubtedly — perhaps by a professional. This slayer had style: .25 cal automatic pistols were uncommon, and almost chic. They were compact, concealable and unlikely, when used, to spray blood or tissue on the surroundings, the killer often being a part thereto and hardly desiring any evidence to adhere.

Was this man fussy or fancy, or was it a heartless woman, with a grudge?

Hmmm. If one had decided on a planned or 'perfect' murder, Harry concluded that one would *not* use a .25 unless the size of the pistol appealed or was convenient, or, perchance, he had inherited the device. An older pistol too, untraceable by number. Try to buy a new .25 auto these days. The dealers are pushing 9 mm.

Harry loved guns and knew much about them — from old Henry rifles to new Glock autos — but he could not recall *any* revolver made in .25 calibre. Check with Mike on that one. There were tons of .22s in a five or six or seven (!) shot revolver formats, why not a .25 ? No shell casing had been found. What had forensics made of the powder traces? Were there grooves on the bullet? Was a silencer used?

Harry now changed his thoughts, they were only speculative. This choice made more sense: if you wanted a definite kill on the first head shot, you *needed* the .25, because perfect placement of the shot with a .22 was mandatory, and it might require another round and obviate surprise. Both calibers were lethal. The Mob preferred the

.22, it was harder to trace — but — the target could not dash off.

His mind also niggled at *his* uncertainty the tire tracks at both scenes were identical, but the brand was not uncommon. The impressions on back lanes or sandy avenues would, alas, be imprecise. No one had seen the automobile in the case of Mrs. Zlot-kow-ski (whew!) or bug-eyed buck-toothed Beulah. There was a chance the newspaper boy had done, but he was likely eight or nine, and more likely to fancy motorcycles. If he'd been riding his bike it would have been to get home right away and, no! It was too early to savor Christmas, he had not seen the grotesque array in the Plymouth…no, impossible, precluded by the tracks near the house. Confusion!

The lad *had not seen* the corpse!

They would interview him today. Harry wanted to know Willison's enquiries. Mike confessed the man was so brutally huge he just scared the truth out of people. "On this lovely morning, you are just sipping your coffee or orange juice, and wham! on your door, which you open to a shining badge and a truculent face! You, the bystander, freak out!"

Mike's phone call now confirmed what Harry thought: the tire tracks, for all practical purposes, were the same tread, though other brands approximated it, the bullet was a .25, expanded into the frontal cortex, and there were smudges of prints on the driver's door handle and on the steering wheel top. Inconclusive.

"Can you meet me there tomorrow to interview the kid?"

Johnny Gilbert, the newspaper boy, was nine years old and proud of his status. "Except for collection, that's slow, but if you don't get the money the paper don't pay you. I like it when they pay up the newspaper for, like, six months. No collection. You still get tips, mostly at Christmas."

Mike had made the introductions, so Harry asked, "Christmas, big time for you, Johnny?"

"Yup. Santa is going to bring me a BB gun this year, pump, not some dumb lever action. Pump is better."

"I used to have one like that," Harry said. "They're a little more powerful and the BBs don't rattle around in the magazine. If you oil it right, sometimes smoke comes out the barrel."

"Cool." Johnny arranged his newspapers and looked up. "I heard that funny lady over there…" he pointed at the house with its police banner and drew his hand across his throat…"but no body knows who did it."

"Did you know her well?"

"No, she left the money out, I never got to talk to her, officer. Maybe saw her once."

"Have you spoken about this to your customers, John?"

"Heck, no, officer. I got my route planned so I can toss the paper onto their porch or lawn, or, if I have to, put it in the mailbox. They done away with the newspaper boxes, that was OK with me. You had to stop and put the paper in. Now I can do my route in 'bout half an hour."

"Do you remember anything about yesterday? Did you see a strange car, or a stranger around Mrs. Braintree's house?"

"Nope. I rode by her house and tossed her paper up, but that was after they put the yellow banner on the posts and the ladies in white jackets were lookin' inner car."

"But," Harry murmured, "before that?"

"Just one man drove by, a lot earlier, on my way home from school, he was nice. He rolled down his car window and told me Santa Claus was coming to town. I thought maybe he was a secret agent."

Mike asked, "What made you think that?"

"He just looked kind of important. He drove a big ole car, but I dunno what kind. The kind secret agents drive. He looked like the principal of my school. But only sorta. He had sunglasses on and dark hair, slicked back. That's all I saw. Of course, there was the UPS truck later and some of the neighbors comin' home, but I know all of them."

"Do you remember anything about the car, like, the color?"

Johnny thought, but shook his head. "Dark and shiny. Like a limousine. Real big. But I was going the other way. He slowed down and said the Christmas thing and drove off."

"Could you tell how old he was?"

Johnny smiled, "Old, like you guys. But not *too* old."

Mike went on, "If you saw him again, would you recognize him?"

Johnny shrugged his shoulders, "Maybe. If he was in the same car. I want to help the police, but it just is hard. I wasn't lookin' to look."

Mike handed Johnny his card, patted him on the shoulder, and gave him a five dollar bill. "If you see him again, make sure you call *me*, OK?"

"Wow!" said Johnny. "Do I have to tell my mom about this?"

"Just show her my card, and tell her what we discussed. You don't need to mention the five bucks, that's our secret."

"Wow!" Johnny echoed himself, "Wow!" He rode off, one hand on the bike, one hand holding a newspaper. They watched him pedal down the road and fling the paper in a hook shot over his head to a pine-shaded home out of view.

Bozo Willison shrugged his shoulders very differently than had the news boy. "These people, most of 'em are brain dead, no joke. See nothing, hear nothing. The only ones in sight of the road were asleep or just not very observant. One was deaf, or seemed to be. Here's the list."

"OK, Boze, you can go. Stop off at the Dollar Store and ask about the lady and her Santa Claus parade. I should have told you that yesterday."

"It's Harry's fault," said Harry.

Willison tipped his hat and got into the marked police car. He roared off and both men realized how easily dust flew on that byway. "I hope forensics took a sample," Mike said, brushing off his shoulder.

Harry wasn't in the blast and laughed. "This looks to be very slim indeed."

Mike felt a twinge of envy. His friend was tall, handsome, broad-shouldered, and suave. Harry's sunglasses were his Florida necessity, and Mike wished he could afford such a pair. "Two rotten murders in as many days. There goes my life of ease." He imagined Harry as the epitome of grace. Were all Ivy Leaguers so…cool?

He stamped his foot. "Tell me about Yale," he said at last, blank with frustration.

"OK, but over a drink."

They were obliged to go to the B-Ballers as part of the investigation. Of course, Harry would pay, Mike would retain the receipt and turn it in as an expense, of which Harry suspected much but knew naught. Doing one's expense report at the Police Office was called "creative writing." But if Harry solved the crime, as before, at the Yale Club killing, Mike would have to buy him the dinner of his choice.

Harry sat down near the framed Larry Bird poster while Mike interviewed the barkeep. Five minutes later came two frosty beers, which appeared bubbly-fresh, as if they had jumped out from an advertisement. He knew Harry disliked most major American brands, so he'd chosen Beck, on draft, which was supposed to be 'German'. At least Harry was no health food nut who wanted a Perrier, those often cost more. "Can you tell my choice?"

"Light German, probably Beck. They wouldn't serve Lowenbrau here. This is not so bad. When you're thirsty."

"Learned very little. There were a lot of customers and Louie the Barman remembered the Braintrees because they were regulars. There were at least twenty others, he said, several were single men, but he knew none of them. All paid by cash. Most of these places don't take plastic, but if they know you, you can have a tab and pay each month. Louie told me that before. He rarely talks to his customers and never socializes with them. Not that kind of place. And, Louie's not all that bright. Even if he knew, he wouldn't remember, even less, get involved."

The name 'Louie' got Harry going on their projected theme of Yale. "From the tables down at Mory's, to the place where Louie dwells..." which he sang *sotto voce*. That was about as 'Yale' as one could imagine, although he had gone to Mory's just three or four times. It was almost kitschy and always too expensive in times when he had no money. Justly famed, though. It impressed people, but so did George and Harry's, an old cafeteria; he wondered if that time-honored place still thrived. Restaurants did surprisingly well in New Haven, competing more with Yale food than each other.

The institutional food at Yale was known to be the best, it was run by a little old lady who had an office near Commons, and who bought potatoes, for example, by the railway car load. For an appointment with her, you had to wait weeks, and, *you* had to go to *her* office!

"Mike, Yale is not an easy mouthful. When I went there it was the finest liberal arts university, as Harvard pretty well stuck to science. I studied English with the great Harold Bloom, who is now a best selling author, even though he is a critic, though a charismatic one. Whereas New Haven was a drab city run by a Democratic machine, our Mother Yale was set apart, and we all had to dress in tie and jacket, no blue jeans. I was back last year. Things have changed."

Mike offered, "I don't wear blue jeans myself. Makes you look stupid. Like a Red Chinese peasant. I don't mind Lee type jeans in tan, they wear well. They tried to make the Detective Bureau wear suits, but we didn't. Who wants to look like an FBI agent?"

Harry heard him — superficially. He went on, "We had some of the most brilliant minds in many fields, such as Chinese history and English, my major, and French. Hell, almost every department! There was the Yale Medical School, the Forestry School, the Divinity School — those "folks on the hill" — the Art School, which included Architecture, and the Drama School, attended by Rock Hudson and that wonderful young actress, Meryl Streep. Keep your eye on her! Our only embarrassment was the School of Nursing and Midwifery, but they were useful on the weekends, for 'horizontal refreshment.' But the school included them by name at graduation!Can you believe that?"

He waxed nostalgic. "There were many rich kids but no fraternities, save for one, I don't remember its appellation. When you go to Yale, you attend a residential college, unless you're in another one of the 'schools'. When you graduate, you also get a degree from your college. I never used to say 'I went to Yale' I would say my college name, 'I went to…'"

"OK, Harry. Thanks for the tour. So here you are in Florida, divorced, with no kids, driving one helluva Mercedes, and helping out a crazy Irish cop with a Jewish father. Mother of God and Saint Isidore, bless us one and all! As for Yale, don't you guys sing Boo-Boo, something like that?"

Harry waited for that rare pause but the detective kept tapping his fingers on the table. He imagined Fenno Heath hopping in anger. "Mike, if you visit New Haven, by all means go to the Beinecke Rare Book Library. It has walls of thin marble that the sun shines through, and, an original Audubon and…hold your breath…an original Gutenberg Bible."

"Ain't that great! I'm burning with envy!" He put down his empty glass. "Why did I invite this topic? Let's hit the road, if you don't mind."

"Did you find out anything about the stretch limo at the country club?"

"Not yet. They're just as common there as…that brand of tires. Rich dicks, the lot of them, with a babe in tow. Who knows, recreational druggies too?"

"What about the chauffeur of the limo?"

Mike stared at Harry directly. "No, that's one I forgot. They're commonly former pimps or pushers who know their way around town. Good idea. A loose end."

Harry left money on the table. "My sentiments exactly."

10

The Man had retired after making his list and thinking on it. He decided not to murder a woman this time. Was society not more sympathetic to them than it was to men? Were they ever prosecuted as ruthlessly as were men at court? Don't we all feel women are our mothers, more or less? Their tears and tumults — somehow — exonerate them from blame. But a low down male, a waif, a…?

He *would* find a pimp, he knew, but he did not want to use the .25 automatic. Ballistics experts might have trouble with an exploding bullet, yet, the Man did not want to take that chance and be repetitious. He countered himself with an objection that pimps are often shot, or stabbed, but it still wouldn't do, though he'd take the .25 along for protection.

Over the years he had assembled an armory of sorts, various tools for slaughter. A long stiletto, a Bowie knife, a Spanish made rapier which hung on his wall, a replica tomahawk with a razor edge, and several clean hypodermics wrapped in sterile plastic. He decided on the latter as his main instrument. For backup, he would bring the stiletto. If necessary, he could use the twenty-five. He held the hefty Bowie knife and shook his head. To be donated to the VFW.

He now took two syringes, filled one with a mild solution of cocaine, and the other with cyanide. To go with that, a supply of marijuana in three small bags, and crack crystals, that rattled in a prescription bottle. Next step…next step…*next step?!*

His wonderful car, *that* would raise some eyebrows on MLK Boulevard. He could, if necessary, use his alternate plate, skillfully affixed to the back of his regular one, and held magnetically. A plate from Georgia with papers to match. So, his Cadillac was showy…so much the better! Camouflage in plain sight.

Money, money, money! He counted out ten crisp fifty dollar bills, touching only their edges and put them into a bank envelope, the half-size you got from the teller, then tucked that into his jacket inner pocket, and the needles into the left outside pocket, drugs in the right. He decided to keep the .25 in his waist holster. He wanted this killing to be almost hygienic, and certainly, without a hitch.

Perfect! Perfect! Perfect!

The Man wanted, above all, to be close to the victim, and savor each painful death throe. How long the agony lasted would depend on how carefully he seduced and killed the procurer. A challenge to vaunted street wisdom!

Utterly famished, he drove downtown, obeying all laws, to his favorite restaurant, where he ordered a Surf and Turf. The Man deemed it necessary to have a protein reserve, he made a fuss with the waitress on how to cook the steak, and that he wanted extra drawn butter for his lobster tail, well, could he have an extra one? Of course, they were just so much. Were they local, from chicken lobsters, or were they from South African stock? "Thank you, thank you, very much!" How peckish he could be!

He'd not eaten for two days, having slept most of the time. Sleep, though, was a kind of food. He'd also enjoyed his morning's newspaper's terse version of Beulah Braintree's death, on the second page, so, he figured, the cops wanted to downplay it. Nothing about Zelda. Most killings in the city had been drug-related and usually gruesome though no one would mistake Beulah's murder for such. Shotguns, machine pistols, heavy calibers, Dirty Harry and the like. The American way! Shoot 'em good and dead!

"I shot a man in Reno, just to watch him die…" Junkies of the world, unite! Smile, Death, your bleak smile. I love You, I am your servant, just watch me, God of Blood and Sorrow! I come with Your blessing! At supper first, in touch with the Higher Reality.

He asked the waitress for an afternoon newspaper which she brought just before the food. He looked at last in the obituaries, but neither victim was there. One must call that a 'hiatus.'

Which did not entitle him to a drink, however; he wanted to be cool as his cucumber salad. He chose ginger ale which would be his champagne. He ate extravagantly but slowly, it was so good! The bill came to thirty-four dollars, and, telling the waitress how scrumptious the food and her service were, he plucked a fifty from his coat.

"Keep the change."

In the unlit parking lot he was careful to brush off his garb with a clothes brush, fancy, made in England, which he kept in the car. A boar's bristle for his coif bore it company, and with that hairbrush he neatened himself. He might get a trim tomorrow, and have it cut short. Did the boy on the bicycle remember his style? That was unlikely. Moreover, the shorter haircuts, like a brush or a flat-top, would create a new identity, for the next victim, after the dispatch tonight. "Officer, the killer was middle-aged, and close cropped…".

Hah, ha!

The light traffic, on a full stomach, permitted him to enjoy the endless variety of city lights. He felt as if he were going to a Broadway show. Animated neon signs, the glamorous spots on Byzantine or Romanesque buildings, the soft pink illumination of a famous night club, until, driving contentedly, and loving even the Christmas colors of traffic lights, save for the brief orange, he came to the honky tonk shade and flicker of MLK Boulevard.

It was just after dusk, and he saw a few whores, colored girls decked in sparkling rhinestones or egregious sequin moirés. One had tight-fitting slacks that showed superb buttocks, and another wore a sweater that outlined voluptuous breasts. When he slowed down, they noticed the car, tentatively came by, but he did not solicit them. He watched for a pimp, most likely a Negro with a broad brimmed hat.

Never deal with *any* pimp who can't afford a big hat and with a swaying plume attached! Now who said that?! He shook with excitement, he said aloud, "'Twas me!" Then, in heavy anticipation, he decelerated, breathed easy: "Stop talking to yourself!"

Under a street light there was at last his man, an ebon Cyrano de Bergerac with the requisite hat, even a *panache*, and, the Man was pleased to note, he was dressed in a tasteful tailor-made gray suit. That would be his ticket, that be the Boss of the Block.

He slowed down his car, almost to a roll in NEUTRAL, and the man perked up. Slowly approaching, stealthy, like a black panther, he stopped close to the curb, just beyond the cone of light from a street lamp. The pimp had been talking to a night-lady, but she walked off with an angry swaying of her hips. The Man pressed an illuminated switch which made the passenger window roll down.

The fellow came up, and the Man could see his gold watch, his gold tie clip, and when he smiled, the gold and diamonds in his teeth.

"Kin ah help you, Sir?"

"Yes. I'm new at this sort of thing. I want a woman for tonight, and I want to take her home, not to some cheap hotel."

"You a cop?"

"Of course not!" He laughed. "I've never been asked *that* before *and* I've never paid for sex *before*, but my friend Charlie said *this* was a good place to come."

"Sure, I know Charlie. Good customer, that dude."

Sure, sure, he "knew Charlie", because the Man did not, a fiction, he knew, just baloney! At least the Man had found a true entrepreneur. With a deep breath before asking: "Do you mind getting in? I don't want to be seen here talking with you. I just want a woman." He took out a fifty dollar bill. "Here's for your advice."

The face beneath the hat came half-way into the window. He could see the pimp had a mustache and a carefully trimmed goatee. When the Negro saw it was a fifty dollar bill, he paused, and got in the Cadillac. The light did not go on when the door was opened, the Man had set it that way but the fella seemed not to notice. He took the money and sat back. With a touch on the switch the window rolled smoothly up.

"Fine upholstery, Sir. Soft leather, I'll bet these seats are heated. Whatchu pay for these wheels?"

"Lots. This car was custom built. Did you see that movie with James Bond, with the seat that shoots out in the air? You're sitting on it."

The black man laughed. "You shittin' me." He tapped the felt ceiling. "How'm supposta go through this roof? Man, you gotta strange sense of hoo-mur." He tucked the bill inside his shirt, which the Man saw was made from yellow silk. "Look, Sir, with all due respect, a good woman for all night costs *more* than fifty bucks...."

The Man extracted another fifty and handed it over. "I don't expect something for nothing. My friend Charlie said it would cost a few hundred."

"Charlie be right," the Negro returned. "There's all kinds of way to pay, though. Cash, always, but some girls likes to do a few lines, some likes high class catered food, some makes you wear a Trojan..."

"What's your name?"

"*Sheeit*, my name is Amos, like Amos and Andy. What be yours?"

"Just call me Charlie, if you want." They both laughed.

The Man was glad to feel a sudden revulsion rising in his gut, pure racial hatred, he was now eager to just shoot the pimp, and push him out the door, but that wouldn't work. He put the car in gear and started driving.

"Where we going?"

"Amos, I can't stand this neighborhood. We'll drive around. When I explain my needs, we'll stop and you can dial up your floozy. Then we'll pick her up, whatever you say…however it works."

"Sure, boss. I got several ladies in mind. I take it, you're looking for black pussy. It's the best kind."

"That's my idea, Charlie told me so. I'd like a woman with a big bottom and big bosoms. Short hair, not too much make up, and not over thirty. Maybe she should have shaved herself, you know, down there…"

Amos laughed and slapped his knee. "That's the coming trend," he said. "Don't ask me why. It ain't pussy without hair, that's my view. But can be arranged." He giggled and added, "Ah used to be a ladies' barber." They both laughed again.

"Don't get me wrong but I heard colored woman have lots of hair, and it's like steel wool."

Amos now guffawed. "Sure, that's an old joke. That's why niggahs don't eat pussy, bad for the tongue, tear yo' lips off." He reached to turn on the radio but the Man said, "No. Leave it off. I want to get the details right on this. By the way, I got some Columbia Gold and a few ounces of powder." He reached in his pocket and took out one serving of cocaine. "Here, this will show I'm serious. I want a real good time."

The antipathy inside him swelled. He had always seen blacks at a distance, harmless and cute. Jiving as they walked. Now up close, he detested them. Amos opened the bag, licked his finger, touched the powder, and tasted it. He smiled broadly, and put some in his nose, which was broad, flat, and possessed of huge nostrils. As Amos sighed with satisfaction, the Man wanted to scream : *"You goddam dirty nigger, you black son-of-a-bitch, you shit-colored nig-nog…I hate your guts and your black ass. You people are all gorilla shit…go back to Africa where you belong…"*

Never had the Man felt such visceral hatred. All he wanted to do was take out his stiletto and drive it home. But he did not. He had to drive.

He said only, "Good stuff, huh?" He kept the Caddie at an even moderate speed, and turned corners, always to the right, so they returned, more or less, to where they had been before.

"Charlie, I beginning to like you. You got money, a nice car, and extra ballast, as we say. You and I gotta smoke a woolah together, that being a reefer soaked in coke. You up for that?"

"I got a better idea. You keep that coke for later, I'll give you the Columbian Gold, which is not generous, as I don't 'inhale'. I got a lot more stuff at home. Nice apartment with a nice view and a super big color TV." He found a dark patch on the side street and pulled over.

Their faces were illuminated by the extensive dashboard in the Cadillac, and he could see Amos smiling confidently to himself. *Caught him a real good sucker this time.* "Hold on," he said and took out the syringe with the mild solution. "I'm crazy for coke, just like you. But it's ten times better from a needle."

He switched on a small spotlight overhead which focused on his right arm. Then, he pulled up his sleeve and inserted the needle, giving himself half the dose. Breathing heavily, he said, "I don't get much of a kick from it otherwise." He could vaguely see Amos scrutinize the syringe. "Think I'll save the rest for later."

Amos pulled his hat back and extended his legs. "You be a *very* different dude, Charlie. You wants to give more than you wants to take."

"Do me a favor, put it back in the wrapper so we can get going."

Amos held the needle up and saw it was dripping slowly, and he held it up to the light and depressed it carefully. The tinge of blood disappeared, and without further comment, he pulled his sleeve up and injected the remainder into his own arm. He was thin-skinned, like many tropicals, and the Man saw so many blood vessels, like tiny winding snakes, he wondered how Amos could choose the right one.

But Amos did, and sat back. He was quiet for five minutes, enough time to switch on the station that played blues and jazz and other such junk 'music' the Man thoroughly detested. In the dim light he could see Amos' expression, it was dreamy yet dissatisfied. Amos, he hoped, he had planned, would need another hit.

"It's gonna cost you another two hundred, that is, if you give me the grass and some more powder. But with all due respect, that injection was fairly weak, I guess you be a newby with the dope…"

He pretended to put the car in gear, and then to return it to PARK. "I have to drive this car and it's the kind of buggy the cops look out for, to write a nice juicy ticket."

"Ain't that the truth!" The pimp readjusted his hat and extended his legs. "They keep telling me this fedora going out of style!" A brief chuckle. "Ah doan think so. My own mother picked it out fo' me."

The Man almost burst into a hoot of laughter, but he stopped himself, and said calmly, "I've a got a full strong needle for later, it's right there." With a pickpocket's sleight of hand, the Negro held it up. "Ah noticed that in the package befo'. Is this one we be sharing?"

"No, when you get the girl, you can take it along…on the house."

A police car drove by them but kept a steady velocity as it passed.

"Don't worry, these windows are hard to see through, heavily tinted. As you might guess, I like privacy. And, the Florida sun can heat up this auto like you don't believe."

Amos reassured him. "Cops doan bother me, they be on the payroll. Pay 'em with pussy sometimes. Now, with due respect, I'm just going to use this dose right now, 'less you object."

"As long as you get me a nice girl. But leave some for me. I'm game."

Amos took the needle and injected himself again, as if he had a Ph. D. in phlebotomy. He lurched back rigidly and said *"Ahhh...!"* then he went rigid and was quiet. His legs kicked briefly and his head hung forward and the Man knew, knew blissfully, that Amos was dead. Amos had expired almost at once, depriving him of an elongated thrill, but he'd given a thrill nonetheless. Brief as an orgasm with a winsome wench.

The small bulb in the Caddie gave the Man the light he needed. He removed the needle and inserted the previous syringe emptied of cocaine. Then, he pulled the man's hat down, and stroked back the huge feather on it. Amos looked asleep, in a bad dream. A touch on his neck showed no pulse. The Man felt electricity when he touched the cool black flesh. He hallucinated that the pimp Amos was faking, would awaken, and, cursing maniacally, plunge a knife into his side.

He lifted the man's lean left arm and it fell back. Once more, he lifted it, and it dropped back the same way, with a smooth pendulum motion. Death so quick! He thought cyanide was supposed to take longer.

"Time was now of the essence," his brain rehearsed, time in breaths and pounding heartbeats, time that could *not* appear on a clock's face…he was so enthralled with the success of this murder, Time had left him fairly faint, yet he wanted to get up and dance, he wanted…

The return of the police car shocked him into a frozen pose, but, although it slowed down, it did not stop.

If they had seen Amos inside, they might have done. He was sure the cops could recognize his car again if they saw Amos in it, but how could they see inside? He almost began a prayer, but, at last he went limp, breathed normally, and began to think.

Someone in this dark ghetto must have noticed, so I must get out, I must put Amos in the churchyard, in the potter's field...somewhere!

That was a part of his plan he forgot to formulate, where to put his victim. It astonished him, three murders and he was turning sloppy, slipping, falling, failing. There was no way to export the body nearby, even if he pretended to help a drunk on some bench. He could not open the door and roll Amos into the gutter. He could not bring Amos home and dismember and bag him (he laughed on this) nor put him into a steamer trunk for deposit at the railway station. How he wished that seat were a James Bond gizmo, now that would be helpful. Push the button and old Amos would be shot into the sky! But to flip, flop and land...where?

Time pecked on his brow. He did not want Amos to begin the excretions associated with death, urine and the rest, not on his gorgeous leather seat. This caused him, perversely, but for a moment, to repent having killed the Negro in the first place, but that tender erratic emotion was short-lived. Amos was a nigger pimp and had to be left where his body would arouse no busybody to report it.

When he fixed the needle into the arm of the corpse, he knew, as he rolled up the sleeve, then put the Cadillac in gear...he knew!

There was a small bridge on his way home, used mainly by cyclists, and, after dark, by amorous pedestrians; it led to an exquisite beach. Underneath flowed a current of some force, said to reach the Atlantic.

So, carefully, honoring all traffic signs and signals, he drove to the bridge, stopped in the middle, and, grateful for its smallish guard rails, eased the body of Amos the Pimp over them, into the dark flow, wherein it splashed, hat and all.

11

"Sorry to drag you to breakfast again, Harry, but I need your observation point on my review…"

Harry never minded the meeting or the feeding of Mike, he still yearned to catch the murderer, to thwart his genius. He wanted to prevent a plague. This morning's paper had sensationalized both killings, and implied that a "deranged serial killer" was on the prowl. "They didn't get that from me," he said, handing the paper to Mike.

"Possibly from our colleague, Bozo Willison. Nothing stops leaks, not even oatmeal. I spoke to Mrs. Zlotkowski's lawyer yesterday, nothing remarkable there. Death certificate on order. Am I saying that name right?"

"My Polish expertise isn't much, but I think it's '*Zwot*-kow-skee'. They don't say 'God' they say 'Bog'. It's a tongue twister."

"The leak may be a good thing," Mike continued, "these muckrakers flush out leads, about twenty bad for one good, but the latter we cherish."

"Cream for your coffee?" asked the waitress. Her cleavage invited an earthy response, but both eyed her, then each other, and smiled.

Mike said "Yes, miss, but I'm supposed to be lactose intolerant."

"Oh, that's nice," came the sweet voice. "But it's better to be open-minded."

The evidence was mostly confirmations of previous estimates. Zelda Zlotkowski was run over by a large auto, not a truck, and the tires were expensive Goodyears, popular in Florida. No one on her "block" had seen or heard a thing. If Harry hadn't come along, she might have lain there for hours. The diamonds were diamonds, altogether worth $10,000. Zelda was in excellent health before being crushed and crumpled.

In the Braintree case, partial fingerprints from the right hand were found, but too small and too smudged to be of forensic value. The footprints were inconclusive but adjudged to be narrow size nine and a half, with slightly pointed toes. The .25 bullet was extracted but had exploded into pieces, no good ballistics there. Powder residue suggested CCI as the maker of the shell. No relevant fibers found. Because older people suffer *rigor mortis* sooner than the young, time of death, two to three hours before discovery, and after 2:32 p.m., the time on the store receipt. The UPS delivery had come at 6:31 p.m. "or so," according to the driver, who didn't take much notice of Beulah in her car, as he was behind schedule. However, the odd Santa Claus look caught his attention and convinced him of foul play.

"At least we have *some* time frames," Harry offered. "If the murderer was the same person, he would have gone straight to lunch at the B-Ballers, or else, have been waiting for Beulah to come home. That's a toss up. Too tight."

"Agree," said Mike. "I don't like the idea that the killer dashed off to the restaurant to start a series. That's too 'optimistic'. You found Zelda at eleven and your tee time was supposed to be eleven fifteen. We might — painstakingly — find a description of him from other diners. Beulah's brother has no recollection of any other diner, kindly note. His back was to the premises, she sat against the wall. When he left, he just wanted out and to get clear. He came to the office this a.m. and went over the events. But, he claimed to go off in a huff, because he didn't want to take Beulah to the track, shopping or to a movie in the first place. Bob Braintree noticed little, cares less, and he's no eagle-eye."

"When you were talking with Louie, I counted the seats in that room. At max, only thirty people could have been there, and as it was busy that day, wouldn't it be less likely for Braintree to have noticed, I mean, if there are only two people sitting next to you in a restaurant, you'll remember them. When there are many, you ignore them. Right?"

"Good point, Harry. That bar has a mixed clientele, some from up north, and many from this area. It's not a local hang-out, like Dinky's, where *everybody* knows *everybody*. Louie serves his guests from the bar, and that abuts the kitchen. No waitress, no witness."

"My kingdom for a wench!" The waitress was nearby and smiled. She liked Harry, so did most women.

But, sidling over, she fairly whispered in his ear, "We don't have wenches on the menu."

"Thank you, Giselle! Now scoot!"

Mike once more regarded Mr. Saybrook with envious eyes. "You go out with her, Harry, and you'll have your hands full."

"I only date dumb blondes, not dumb brunettes. She is sweet. Full figured, fabulous! Seriously, we either have a newborn serial killer or we don't. If he has killed in quick succession, he may kill again soon. Possibly a woman, and definitely not a lovely young looker, no, some fading malodorous flower. Do you think he might have a mother complex?"

Mike passed over a report. "I hadn't read this yet. Another killing, but I don't think it's our guy. Read up."

The grotesque photo of Amos the Pimp *sans chapeau* caused Harry to think the fork in his hand weighed a ton. He put it down and went through the report. "Well, did he drown or die of an overdose? You have it as a homicide."

"They found a needle emptied of its cocaine stuck into his left arm, but the coloration of his skin makes them think it was juiced, you know, bad stuff. But somebody dumped him, it seems likely, from the Botany Bridge, just down the road. Because of the tides he didn't float too far from shore. The corpse was wearing a Rolex and other expensive jewelry. So, murder? It must be, without the theft of valuables. I think he was up for a party but chose the wrong sponsor. We had one other pimp go that way, overdosed at some orgy, and left to rot. In the garden of a Eurotrash playboy. They found him lying in a bed of lilies."

"Says here he had a pocket full of cannabis and a bag of cocaine. No other needles. Three hundred bucks, two fifties, the rest in twenties. Do you have a man on it yet?"

Mike nodded and picked up his phone. "Speak of the devil. We have a colored detective who knew 'Famous Amos'. He was the 'high class' pimp on MLK. No relation to the cookie maker. One of his ladies saw him approach a big shiny car, but that's all she saw, as he had dispatched her to a local motel, the Blue Boy, she said. Because of Amos' condition they figure he died around ten p.m. About a hour after the shady lady said 'bye'. She didn't see him get into the car, but sometimes pimps will get in, to check out the prospect or to be ferried to a rendezvous. It was a larger vehicle and shiny, that's all she could remember. But in that neighborhood, pimps and whores often go right up to the car to do business. Let's not go car crazy or Caddie crazy. Cars, of all shapes and sizes, cruise the area, some to look, some to buy."

"I've got that funny little guy from the club on my mind, for no reason." Harry raised his eyebrows and handed back the report. "I'd like to know the exact cause of death. How much forensics do you perform, *on a pimp*?"

"Next to nothing, they're generally not mourned by anyone. Besides a child molester, there nothing in the criminal ranks ranked lower. Lots of pimps get shot or knifed, not because they are procurers, but because they are notorious informers. They do anything for money. A pimp in jail is just a chicken waiting for the axe. But

'Famous Amos' was a cut above the rest, ate and dressed well, and had the biggest hat, with a huge plume. He was also known as 'the Cavalier.'"

"No mention of a hat in the report."

"Doubtless, on sale in some shop, if the salt water didn't ruin it. It was famous! The body wasn't too bloated but it had been at sea for half a day. I once met that crazy guy, Amos, he had, of course, no class, but plenty of style."

"Who found the body?"

"A lifeguard at Botany Beach very early this a.m. It was going out to the ocean, but he brought it in with his lifeboat. Nice kid, I hear. Honest at least, didn't rob the body."

"Besides the cause of death, forensics should check his shoes. Could be something on them. If he had junk on his feet, it could have rubbed off in the culprit's car, or got fibers stuck to it."

Mike looked tired and discouraged. He smiled. "We're having a spate of murder, it often happens here and there. I don't think we can link the three, unless *you* can thread the needle."

"Bad quibble, Mike. He could have done some bad stuff, his friends didn't want to be involved, so they tossed him overboard." Harry was finishing his coffee. "It's just lousy intuition. One death, another…the second having earmarks of a pro. The eerie presence of a big car, maybe on this killing also. Hell, most of what we have down here are big cars, with big air conditioners inside. Well, in the colored neighborhood, someone's always watching, so *someone* saw *something*."

"You got cars on the brain. Me too. I think that's distracting us. That custom built Caddie in the club parking lot. Did that guy strike you as odd or menacing? Let's not chase the wild goose!"

"I didn't really eyeball him, I was looking inside the trunk of his car, where he kept his golf bag. He seemed to want me to see that golf bag, to…distract me."

"Your imagination." Mike brightened. "He kept the trunk open until you left. So, my flatfoot brain says he just didn't want you to see his license plate."

Harry paid the bill and they got up. "Mike, you may be right. You might have hit the nail on its proverbial head."

"Personally," said Mike, "I think I'm full of S.H.I.T."

"More than your candor, Michael, I love your marksmanship." Harry stood up. "Let's go, I think I'll chat with Judge on this."

They went out the back and a breeze snuck in behind them, making the shamrocks dance on their wires, an Irish wiggly jig around the poster of Larry Bird.

12

The Man was deflated. No further news on his two killings; after a sensational spread, nothing about Amos the Pimp. The local newspaper was more interested today in the opening of a new hotel, and the visit of a movie star. He was expecting too much: instant notoriety from three rapid-fire murders. Moreover, he had a business to run, and this neglect unsettled him.

He had to pick up his golf bag at the club. Then, he could reload it with cocaine, and plan another drop off there. This very simple system had worked for a year, when he had joined the club as a charter member. Golf bags had pockets galore, and some had hideaways.

The chauffeur was a Cuban refugee who loved cash and who loved coke. He paid the Man up front and one day later, more or less, he took delivery, usually at the golf club. One bag always had money, the other bag cocaine, and the third was a duplicate meant to confuse.

Maybe they would switch to the posh new hotel, wherever high rollers hung around. Golf bags, with their various pockets, were great delivery parcels. Sometimes the chauffeur, whom he knew as 'Juan', would leave the bag near the clubhouse at an appointed time. It always contained the cash for his next shipment. He did not worry about its security, many such bags were left in a standard row, and were sometimes taken in by the pro shop at dusk, then replaced next day. Only if rain threatened.

In his apartment the Man had a wall safe but kept little money there. He had a fake quart of orange juice and sometimes put his large bills into a waterproof sack. Its yellow hue could not be seen. He kept fresh fifties in his desk, no more than two thousand dollars altogether. His balcony had a hamper, neatly designed to grow marijuana. If he did get busted, the cops would be happy with that, and he could cough up enough cash to send them on their way.

It was time for a brief vacation. He could tour the coast, stop by at Boca, get some fine cuisine, and kick up his heels. He dealt with a real estate lawyer there who invested his monies and who never complained about cash. Very above board too. He'd checked out the paperwork in the registry office, all kosher, like his agent. A charming Jewish lawyer who handled client after client, even Gentiles like himself. Someone had said "they" laundered the money through the charity of "their" local synagogue, but who knew, and who cared? On paper the Man was now worth almost two millions dollars.

He did not want to murder anyone in Boca, because instinct told him he'd not get away with it. No one got away with anything in Boca except Jewish lawyers. Sometimes they were caught. By other Jewish lawyers!

13

Mike had complained of driving so Harry took him to MLK Boulevard in the Mercedes, top down. The bright day revealed the sleazy character of the locale and its many indolent folk; store windows unwashed, litter by the curb, and, here and there, a window boarded up.

Jimmy Johnson was Mike's detective in that precinct. He smiled broadly as his boss pulled up. "*Fan-see*, Mike. Wish I had a nice white boy to drive me 'round like that." They had pulled over, he had skulked up. "Found the lady who saw Amos and the car. She's Blessed Latoya, over in the café." He snapped his fingers and a well-upholstered black beauty sprang to life, and with a jaunty clackety walk on her stiletto heels, joined them at curbside.

She gave Harry a winsome look and then said "Hello" to Mike. "Been busy, babe?" he asked. She just smiled, her teeth resplendent in full lips coated with fuchsia gloss. To Harry, "*You,* I could get to like."

The men chuckled. "OK, Latoya. We love you."
Her charm was ebullient, to say the least, but Latoya
exuded femininity through an hygienic soapy perfume.
She had bathed carefully that morning, she knew cops
were fussy. Whores that smelled bad got treated bad.

"Latoya, what happened? You know, somebody
wasted Amos, and word is, you were his top girl." Mike
made as if he doffed an invisible top hat. "Was that you
getting even?"

"Word be right," she replied, ignoring his
suggestion, half with respect, half with a saucy smirk. "It
was a funny night, he hadn't no calls or nothin' on his
beeper, and we were just watchin' traffic. There was a
bunch of cruisers, some kids, some cabs, and that big
shiny car. But I think Amos smelt a deal and tole me to
leave. Said we would catch up at the Shamrock Hotel,
where we'd had sum fried chicken de night befo'."

"Do you think he got into that 'shiny car'", Harry
asked.

"Dunno. I didn't see it, but it could be. Guys that
drive those fancy cars usually do business inside 'em. The

cheaper customers just pull up and say 'Get in' and off you go, once a price is agreed. That can be dangerous, and I'll miss Amos, because he only sent me the nicest johns."

Jimmy put in, "He treated her good, but she's a good girl. Keeps herself clean and in good shape, never cheats on the fee. Kinda girl you'd bring home to meet Mom."

Blessed Latoya laughed immoderately.

Mike asked, "You just walked off, and all you remember is Amos going up to the car..."

"Yeah, I looked back and now I 'member, he got in. Well, he musta because he kept his head in the window. But the car sat there fo' a while. Nothing for me to survey. I think, cause by then I was off. Went to the drug store for some supplies."

Jimmy said, "Some folks saw that shiny car driving around, staying in the neighborhood, but only one or two legit sightings. Lots of people watchers here, not many car watchers. 'Less you include stretch limos, they always attract attention."

Mike asked, "Were there any?"

Jimmy nodded 'no.'

Harry cast his eyes about, to the pavement, and asked Jimmy, "Is there any local stuff that would stick to shoes?"

"You mean, stick on ole Amos' shoes? Like chewing gum? Maybe rub off on somebody else, somebody's car, somebody's carpets? Local grunge, but I'll get a sample. Something should have stuck to ole Amos' slippers. Forensics gotta check dat."

"Let's not forget he spent more than an hour in the ocean. Salt water is the death of evidence."

"But Mike, it don't wash off certain chemicals. I haven't seen the body, but I hear it's pretty bad. Some bloating, disfiguration. Amos was a nice lookin' guy."

Blessed Latoya started to cry. "He was a good man for all that," she sobbed. "Never hurt me, was nice to most workin' ladies. Now I gotta work for Blut-oh."

"He's *not* so nice," said Jimmy. "Don't confuse him with the Popeye character, this dude's name is Blue-Toe. He wear funny, funny shoes always with a blue toe, that got a steel protector and if he kicked you, you turned black…and blue!"

"You already being black, saved him some trouble," Harry put in.

Latoya tittered, "We're all the same color inside."

Jimmy, still laughing, added, "Yeah, and you girls all be pink in the middle."

"Some be pink, some be orange," Latoya said proudly.

When they had gone their ways, Mike concluded the allusion, "Yeah, when they spread their legs, Harry, it's like a neon light…"

Harry carefully entered traffic. "Ah, the voice of experience!"

Mike showed his companion Jimmy's brief report. "Not much to go on, just this 'shiny car' which is our phantom villain. In a town full of shiny cars and fat tires. Not enough fingerprints to matter, but your suggestion about Amos' shoes could bear fruit. They'll have a go at it today."

"I'm hoping they find some fibers which might identify the car, if the poor bugger got into it. He didn't have to for business, that can be done on the phone. But I don't think Amos went around during work hours with a needle hanging on his arm. That seems neatly arranged, don't you think?"

Mike answered, "I'm sick of thinking and running short on shoe leather. A dead pimp doesn't make the police blotter when a rich widow is being pulped on the road. We don't need a motive on the first, or the third. Let's ask ourselves why someone would kill Beulah Braintree, late of the B-Ballers Sports Bar & Restaurant."

14

The Man's first impression, years ago, of "Boca" was from the mouth of an impoverished Jewish widow with wonderful bazooms. She kept saying the word in a Hebraic chant, through her nose, over and over, so that it was imbued with sexuality, high and low. Maybe it was an

Hebraic chant, or Hindu incantation, but it was certainly not Gregorian. She had infused the word with occasional orgasmic tweets. "Are you Jewish?" she had asked him. He answered, "Sometimes."

After the clubs and restaurants, Boca got dull quickly, unless you knew someone you could play contract bridge with. It helped to be Jewish, and he was not, though was often mistaken as such from his dark hair, dark tan, and neat aquiline nose. He thought he would eventually go north to Palm Beach which was more Anglo, make that Anglo-Phoney. Ethnic differences had lost their savor, there was no salt of the earth, so how should it be invigorated? People were emulating each other, "Oreos", blacks who are white in the middle, "Wannabes", whites who would swim the Congo to get nearer the drum-beats, and many Jews who epitomized Anglo virtues, and after rhinoplasty, resembled them in appearance dispelled only by a Yiddish intonation in their speech. So many younger people had beards, idiotic hair tints, tattoos and piercings, and clothing wearable by either sex, what would the future bring?

He had been tempted to offer a ride to some hippy dippy sorts, but the long-haired Lady of the Lake was often followed by a hirsute companion on her heels, so he was glad of the switch that locked the doors in a split second. You had to drive off quickly as well, often dragging the hitchhiker on the door handle, which was usually fun. But he couldn't see what amusement could come from killing hippies, they were, for practical purposes, already lifeless.

He managed to find a short obituary on Amos Isaiah Varnadore, the Negro he had killed so cleverly. At first he chortled and was gay, then, he felt pity resurface for the man and contempt for himself. 'Famous Amos', as eulogized in the text, was well liked, and no mention of his criminal background appeared. He was a 'local businessman' and left only his mother in Baltimore. The Man thought, however briefly, of having his lawyer set up a memorial fund for 'Famous Amos'. This generous impulse was stifled by his recollection of how thrilled and how satisfied he was to kill the man, and his utter joy of giving that man a watery farewell.

In Boca he had visited the best car wash and paid extra cash for a man to "detail" his car, taking out the carpets, vacuuming the interior, even the trunk, steam cleaning them and wiping off the leather seats with an expensive 'cream'. When the auto was returned he thought it 'better than new' it was splendid, it was so…professional. "Find any odd objects?" he'd asked and had received an honest denial. "I give a lot of folks rides, you know, nice old ladies and cancer patients."

The Negro who completed the task bore an eerie resemblance to 'Famous Amos,' but looked embarrassed at the compliments and the extra gratuity. "You deserve it," the Man said. "You worked hard and did a good job."

As he drove north toward Palm Beach the Man felt his life was accomplished and full. He had made a great deal of money and he had begun an authentic new career, he would amass a variety of victims to add a gleam to his inner glow. It was *so* exhilarating to kill! Was it because one's mark had no idea they were about to die? Was the killer a quirk of fate or fate's destined agent? He was a shark in the waters, invulnerable and insatiable. He would, therefore, swim on and devour as he found, and as he chose.

Traffic flowed nicely, so he could easily review his list from memory. A policeman, eating fried chicken or not, could only be killed in self-defense. Unlikely, undesirable. A real estate agent, they were generally offensive, blind to anything but money. Easy to entrap? Seeing a new house, killing the agent, burying them in the garden…good except most of their appointments were documented. One pimp was enough, perhaps a prostitute next. Someone that knew Amos? Good idea. But not this time. Business man with cigar? Easier said than done.

He took up his valise. It contained all his weaponry except the sword. He thought today or tomorrow he would use the Bowie knife or the replica tomahawk. Not in the mood for a stiletto. Well, who knew, who knew? Late afternoon, time for an early supper.

He was briefly shocked to be waved over by a traffic officer. False alarm. There was a demonstration of students marching in protest and he had been thinking more and driving safely less. The policeman merely held up his hand. Other cars had been stopped and he watched the procession of students, most of whom looked like drop-outs, uncivilized, unwashed, were like a caravansary wandering —where?

His eye quickly discerned a goodly number of dope addicts. They shared a neurasthenic leanness from self-indulgence, certainly not from stoical devotion. Accompanied by some of their professors, they carried neatly lettered placards and banners. STUDENTS FOR…he couldn't be bothered. Talk about an organized protest , subsidized by some Commie cell! He fumed, and decided to make this a stopover.

The marchers found their destination, a small shaded park, where they assembled and peaceably sat down. The Man automatically selected several candidates for death. An overweight lady teacher with roseate cheeks, a thin male prof with a big bald spot but hairy chest and arms, and a normal prof with a normal face who wore thick glasses on his pointy nose and who carried a trombone.

The latter fascinated him. The man was strong but not overly muscular, dressed in chino pants, not blue jeans, and wore a button down Oxford shirt, but no tie. He did not seem part of the protest group but was there, the Man deduced, to make music.

He had parked his car and had taken two bags of Columbian Gold along. By the time he found a place in the park to watch, it was dark, several women students had given speeches, but with the hubbub, he was spared their rhetoric. He plunked down next to a phlegmatic couple who kept saying "Cool" when a protestor stood and briefly ranted. He wondered who could take these people seriously. Nonetheless, he feigned interest and took a bag of marijuana out."Did you drop this?"

The girl, who was at least twenty but looked prepubescent, took the little plastic sac and said, "Huh? Oh, yeah, that's cool." She opened it and smelled the contents. "Hey, man, you sell this stuff?"

"What stuff? You mean that little bag, no, I found it in the grass."

"In the *grass,* ha, ha, that's funny!"

He could see she had no further questions, but elbowed her boyfriend, showed him their trove, and laughed when he pulled out some cigarette papers. "You smoke, man?"

"No, never!" He feigned disinterest. "I just came here to see what you'all are doing. I admire the idealism of youth."

"Cool," said the girl. She lit up the joint and passed it first to her companion, then to another girl in the row. They all inhaled deeply.

"This is good stuff!" The youth took a deep drag. "Sure you won't try this?"

"Cool," said the girl, whose name turned out to be Trudy.

By now the reefer had been passed down the line, to five or six protestors, all of whom rotated their heads in approval. "Good stuff! Cool! Co-lum-bia, gem of the ocean…ha, ha. Gimme another drag. Hey, you got enough for us all…!"

"My name is Jed, what's yours?"

The Man said, "Just call me Charlie. I'm from up north."

Most of the students had driven their placards, which were on neat new staves, into the soft soil. Trudy had rolled another joint and passed it down to the next row. They were nicely regimented, he noticed. Sat in rows but the gathering resembled a powwow, as its participants seemed very "native American" in attire. Trudy had what he thought an expensive beaded band to gather her luxuriant blonde hair into a pony tail suggestive, in its sparkle and shimmer, of a waterfall. She wore a low cut tee shirt that showed the abundant whiteness of her breasts. When she saw he was eyeing them, Trudy giggled, "I just burnt my bra."

As the sun completed its decline, more and more students arrived, and one found a central seat where she began to play her guitar. He did not know the name of the song, but it was easy to sing, some African words, or pidgin French, he imagined. "Good-bye-mah-lawd…goo-bye-ah…".   The chorus was mellow and sonorous, the crowd had reached almost one hundred. The street lights switched on, and of the three police cars, only two remained.

The gaiety seemed to focus below the cloud of smoke generated by his contribution, but, he was sure, many others had brought cannabis along. Some kids were drunk on alcohol, that was obvious from their ostentatious belching. He wanted to disperse the other bag of Mary Jane, but was hemmed in by his coterie of smokers, Jed being their Leader and Jed their chief Gesticulator.

"Who's for peace?" he shouted.

Everyone shouted and clapped their hands. "Who's for love?" Again, applause. Someone behind him said, "Who gives a shit?"

He wondered if some plainclothes policeman lurked in the shadows, but it was a 'normal' kid with short hair and an athletic mien. He was not part of the scene, but held his large can of beer, and looked bored. When the Man scrutinized him the student said, "I came because the Jazz Jingoes are going to play. One trumpet, one clarinet, one sax and one trombone. They're really good."

He liked the young man, smiled, and said, "Cool." He was saluted by a raising of the beer can, and a nod.

It was now dire night, one could see a few stars if one looked away from a small bonfire lit in the center of the gathering. Many might have taken this for a pre-Halloween conflagration. No, it gave a harvest orange light and some warmth to the cool autumn evening. The protest was for Native Indian Rights. He deduced this from a trio of 'braves' who performed a "war-dance", so he was told.

The fire burned bright, and he thought "Florida it does get cold", *sometimes*. He liked the beat of the drums and the pentatonic tunes. His attention had returned to the normal man with his trombone. The firelight played on his thick spectacles so that he looked like a forest priest holding court. His nose gave him a Celtic mien, but he played the trombone extremely well. The Jazz Jingoes were excellent.

The Man had detested "jazz" for years but who knew what "jazz" was? This group had perfected a Dixieland sound with a mad clarinet soprano, a high, witchy sound. Unannounced, it poured out three numbers, and the Man sat back and enjoyed it, figuring that whoever financed the placards and banners might also have paid the musicians. Everyone cheered, and cheered again, when from the shadows a hogshead of beer materialized, with a box that spilled out plastic cups. A ragged line formed and he noticed the cop car just remained at distant curbside, its lights flashing, as before, to deter traffic.

He roved in and out of groups and then near the musicians, who were drinking their share of brew, blowing away the messy suds, swallowing, and refilling. "What was the name of the last piece you played?"

The trombonist, who turned out to be the arranger of the piece, said "Basic Street Blues" or "Basin Street Blues" or "Baskin-Robbins Street Blues," the Man could not tell for the surrounding noise. He sat down next to the trombonist and listened to a brief lecture on jazz, Dixieland jazz, modern jazz, and…the prof went on but he did not listen.

"Just call me 'Alf'" he said, offering his hand. "I'm not part of the march, just here to earn a few dollars with my horn." He explained the slide and how versatile the instrument was, about embouchure, and overtones. The Man handed him a fifty dollar bill and said, "That's part of your comeuppance, from an admirer."

"This must be extra, they told us 'check in the mail' and we accepted that, having done business with them before." He pocketed the money. "Thanks."

"You seem too intelligent to mess around with these hippies," the Man said. "What's this all about?"

"Something about Wounded Knee. At first I thought we were on a medical benefit gig, but it concerns Native Americans."

"My name is Charlie," he said.

"Oh yeah," said Alf. "My main job is professor of European Literature at the, well, you know the college up the road. Pays well but a lot of the students are spoiled, like here."

"Are any of your students here tonight?"

"No, I don't think so. They're mostly serious about their degree. Some of these kids are actually majoring in Swimming Pool Maintenance, can you believe that?"

"It's right up there with Surfing and Scuba Diving." He knew he was going to kill 'Alf', and thought on the opportunity.

Alf finished his beer, laughed, then coughed hard. "This sea air, keeps my lungs busy. Where are you from?"

The Man explained he was tired of the noise, if they didn't have another number right now, let's sit over there, OK, get yourself a beer, good, its dark but you can hear yourself think…

The moment was approaching, he knew that. Alf had relaxed against a tree, and laid his trombone across his gut. He finished his beer and folded the cup, then put it in his pocket. "Hate litter," he said. "Where did you say you're from?"

"I was born in Russia."

"That's more than I can say for myself," Alf returned. "What's your last name?" Darkness surrounded them with night's cloak, and an invisible shroud.

"It's kind of hard to pronounce, but my name is…Raskolnikoff."

Alf was trying to say, "As in Dostoyevsky.." but the tomahawk, heavy steel with its razor edge, flashed down and was buried in his skull. The musician's head flopped forward and blood poured in a stream down his neck.

The Man gingerly took the fifty dollar bill from Alf's pocket, saying "Sometimes one question is too much," and replaced it with his second bag of marijuana. He picked up the trombone. He'd always wanted one and walked out through the back of the park with it barely concealed beneath his coat. He popped his trunk and left it there. His nephew in Michigan would enjoy a fine instrument, so he would send him the trombone by UPS in the morning.

He was about to enter his car when he noticed Jed and Trudy staggering in his direction. "Hey man!" said Jed.

"Cool" he replied. "Cool!"

Still high on the grass, Trudy giggled, high and reedy, like the clarinet that had played all the high notes for the Jazz-Jingo-combo.

15

The party, the protest, had broken up late. The Jazz Jingoes had been paid for merely 'an appearance.' Which was what they gave. Besides a lady folk singer, there were other performers. As no one could find Alf, or, as no one seriously looked for Alf, he remained recumbent where he lay, the shadows of a live oak concealing the native American weapon in his head. At dawn the park attendant found him, but at first left him alone. You couldn't see Alf was dead unless you got up close. Eventually he came round to rouse him, and saw the hatchet in place, as the tree trunk had kept its shaft out of view.

Several people in the protest had been arrested for public intoxication and for possession of drugs to trade. Jed and Trudy were among them. It was an easy bust, and the arresting officer just directed them to the paddy wagon, which marked the end of festivities. Of course this police activity distracted everyone from the murder, and it took two days to identify Alf, as he had no ID and his trombone was missing. Moreover, a bag of high grade cannabis had been found in his pocket. So it looked like a drug deal gone bad, save for the weapon, but that harmonized oddly with the protest theme. When compared with the residue found on Trudy, via a superficial analysis, it was 'identical', though this fact only appeared in a scribble on the coroner's report. A witness at the college attested that Alf was notoriously anti-drugs, but did not refuse a drink. No other conclusions were made. Jed and Trudy were not his students, and did not even know the man by reputation. Alf was a leading light in his field, so gradually, more attention was paid to his demise.

"We heard him play the trombone with the other guys, and we liked the music. You always notice the guy playing a trombone. They didn't play that much. At these rallies there are always some that get up to sing, play, or even tell jokes. And that grass was given to Trudy, she didn't buy it or bring it there."

Trudy told the local officers how a quiet man, well-dressed and friendly, had handed her the drug. She thought he was funny and out-of-place, but she was in a good mood herself and disposed to enjoy any magic gift. "He wouldn't smoke it when I offered him a toke, and he didn't drink the free beer either. I think you'd call him a 'curious bystander', officer."

The other similarity, that the bags were the same manufacture and size, was not remarked upon. Marijuana seemed to come in those bags, and were weighed in such before being sealed for the market by the pusher. The detective suggested that some dope pedlar was circulating in the crowd, and if Alf didn't smoke grass, well, most jazz musicians did. The lieutenant said, "Sure. I remember the story when President Nixon wanted to 'help' Louis Armstrong through customs. 'Could I carry your trumpet?' Later it turned out Nixon had helped smuggle in a week's supply of pot for the band."

The young detective had checked about prints on the tomahawk but there were none, its handle having a tape wound round, that left no useable prints but helped sustain a grip. "Like that pistol in *The Godfather* Michael uses to shoot the cop and Sollozzo. It sure helped that guy drive the blade deep, death in a second. He could of scalped him if he'd chopped that poor bastard on the temple."

Then the lieutenant remembered his pal Mike Herman, up north. A few days later, he forwarded the information with a personal note. "Hear you've had some lulus too."

Mike was secretly rejoicing that no more murders had come his way for almost two weeks. Two victims had been buried and one junior detective kept watch, on and off, near both scenes of crime. He hoped to turn up new evidence, but was treated to the rampant blue jay in one spot, and the happy-go-lucky newspaper boy in the second. As time passed, the murders seemed more and more unrelated.

It was the killing of 'Famous Amos' that came into better focus. The cause of death was not drugs, but cyanide, and that removed any accidental flavor to the crime. The pimp had last been seen in Blacktown, and his body found miles away. Ergo, he was killed in the 'car' and dumped off the Botany Bridge. All of which spoke of method, and that spoke of premeditation. The long shot possibility that Amos was murdered in some apartment, or house, or garage, *and then* transported to the bridge, was considered but not taken seriously. Reason being that a few rare carpet fibers adhered to the sole of the shoe on his left foot.

"I should have thought of that, Harry, not you." Mike had a desk full of notes and reports, and Harry, dressed as usual in tweed and Oxford, shiny Florsheims and his Serengheti sunglasses, sat next to him in the office. As cop shops went, it was well-appointed. The furniture was of polished wood, and the atmosphere was almost Victorian. "Baroque" was Harry's term.

"We cannot identify the carpet fibers except to say they are of higher quality and use the same dyes as in a Rolls Royce. That's a guess. Of course it makes me think of that fabulous Cadillac in the club parking lot and its mysterious driver. But something in my dark subconscious says the connection is imaginary. Should we happen to see that auto parked or accessible, we have enough to look inside without a warrant. There is no requirement to inspect or validate a car which has had improvements. Only if you change the color. As for Cadillacs, new or rebuilt or restored…in this area they outnumber Volkswagens!"

"My friend Judge Rugh and I chatted with the pro shop manager and the groundskeeper the other day." Harry stretched out his legs. "There is a bag rack maintained more by caddies — no pun intended — than in the shop itself. People leave their bags on the last tee and the caddies put them away if requested, or leave them in the general rack on the first tee, where they are protected from the rain. We spoke to several caddies who explained that they could walk the customer and carry his bag, drive the golf cart, or just get the bag and put it in the cart. In the last instance they don't get a fee, just a tip. But the time spent is minutes. There are a few anonymous bags, sure, but most of the caddies can tell you the owner's name if you point to the bag. But I wager, not all."

Mike tapped on his blotter. "How is Judge doing?"

"Loping along with us other bachelors." Harry thought of his ex-wife, Louisa French Saybrook, once his *raison d'être*, and now a *belle dame sans merci*. Then he wondered why Mike never mentioned a girlfriend.

Miss Petton, his secretary, chimed into his thoughts, "Mr. Saybrook, how nice to have you stop by!"

Mike tried to wave her away, but she loved to fawn over Harry, perhaps to annoy Michael Herman, who, if he followed Irish protocol, might marry by the age of forty. "What do you think of these horrible killings?" Harry replied.

Hillary laughed. "Which one, which ones? There are so many!"

"Well, do you think there is more than one serial killer, or a flock of beginners?"

"The first one was an accident, I'm sure. The 'killer' might have been venting his or her hatred. The second is certainly some old enemy of Ms Braintree, or perhaps her brother had her done in for insurance money." She handed Mike the memo. "We just got this in, she was worth two hundred thousand on the slab."

"Continue," said Harry.

"I would disregard that murder of the procurer on MLK. They're getting beaten and blown away all the time. Seems it had a clever touch, though."

"Check this one out, see if it fits…your theory," said Mike, handing her the dossier on Alf the Trombonist.

She sat down on Mike's desk and left her skirt somewhat awry, and Harry "looked." "Admiring my ham hocks?" she enquired.

"Please," Mike injected, "this is a kosher agency."

Which gave Harry time to reply: "Mesmerized at a glance, but now wondering if there was a sexual angle to these…executions."

Hillary put down the papers. "This crime is nothing like the others. Out of our territory, out of profile. Using a tomahawk at a protest rally for Native Americans, that's a bit much. Was this guy Alf gay?"

Harry and Mike both enjoyed the music in her voice, light and lilting. "There were drugs in the last two crimes, which might link them. Women in the first two, could be some Mommah's boy with big ideas. All four seem highly professional or damned lucky. Virtually no evidence," Harry offered, "that counted."

Mike kept a cold eye on Hillary and she left, somewhat ruffled. "She wants to join the DB and I'm almost inclined to let her. But she won't do the preliminaries, to wit, the Police Academy, the uniform, the protocol. Time on the beat."

"Women have an intuitive advantage over us, Michael. Sometimes they can see through what we haven't glimpsed. I'm beginning to see these murders as part of a pattern rather than the work of a serial killer, what do you think of that?"

Mike crossed his legs and tilted back in his chair. "Not much. I'm getting needled by the strange fibers on 'Famous' Amos' shoes. If they were on his left shoe, then he was getting into a car, whereas if they came from a posh apartment the same fibers would be on both feet."

Harry asked, "Weren't there any other such fibers on his person, his clothes?"

"No, thanks to the salty Atlantic brine. The fibers stuck to his shoes because he had similar guck on both feet, doubtless street grime from MLK."

Harry laughed, "I can see the headline: CRIME SOLVED BY UNDISSOLVED GRIME".

"You may just be right, Mr. Saybrook, graduate of Yale. Go have another talk with Judge Rugh, your partner in crime. My guts tell me he has thought over this, and may have further conclusions."

Miss Petton waved and wailed, "Come back soon!".

Judge was at the same table at the golf club. "I've been thinking about it also," he said, after Harry's resumé. "It's a bunch of junk."

The waiter brought the same sparkling beer in frosty mugs. "I feel, and that's miserable logic, many of the pieces fit together, but we need some fulcrum to lift them all into light."

"You have — if you include this trombone player — four murders with four different m.o.'s. Might that not suggest four killers, or, one with an original streak?"

The last murder was far afield, Harry explained. It was appropriate to the circumstance, tomahawk in powwow. "If this manslayer is calculating, would he have known about the protest meeting? It wasn't publicized. Unless he's affiliated with that college. Is he trying to spread a net so wide we cannot intercept him? Now, if we link the female killings on a sexual basis, next we have two male killings, and that supposes they are all linked, which tickles no one's fancy. The only thing I know for sure, it is a man we hunt."

Judge nodded. "All right, the first death was accidental, the murderer did not plan it, or, if he did, he's too smart for us and will escape. Shortly thereafter, another murder takes place, of another woman. Was there some...pregnant seed? Like, 'I killed this 'un now I'll kill me another'?"

"I drove down Zlotkowski Lane *by chance*. Then to the club. To meet you."

"Right. But mightn't that be another overlapping circumstance? What if the killer *were* that funny guy in the big car who showed you his golf bag in the voluminous trunk? OK, a huge supposition, but another working hypothesis. The reason I mention it is that he would never know you had witnessed his crime, but he tried to remain innocuous by letting you see his trunk was empty, save for the golf bag, which also prevented you from reading his license plate, which might have had a memorable custom title, not just Florida alpha-numeric."

"It's one theory that sounds sound, so continue."

"Back to basics. We were late for our tee time, and watered at the bar. We could see the first tee and that it was empty. Theoretically if the man had come here to play golf, he would have gone there. But we ended up getting a cart and our bags and had a reasonable nine holes. Right?"

"I'm waiting for the next circumstance."

Judge burped. "Bring that up again and we'll vote on it!" Pause. "OK, if he opened the trunk to get his bag, and you happened along, he had some use for the bag, but it was not to play golf. Therefore he must have left it in the bag rack with other often anonymous players' sacks of clubs. Or, he could have given it to the driver of the stretch limo, although neither of us saw much of that lot. We'd have to assume the driver was there, waiting, but that can't be checked. Not enough traffic that day."

Harry remembered Mike's advice, consult with Judge Rugh. Judge often had nothing to say about a recent felony, and just as often, could see through a labyrinthine drama. It was a slender and tenuous thread. He told Judge he hadn't given the stretch limo a second look, and that the golf bag in the customized Caddie was nondescript. But so was the man! "It's all too vague. But maybe it's *meant* to be."

Judge finished his beer and, true to form, wiped his mouth on his jacket sleeve. "Harry, I *intuitively* think if you want to bag the murderer, you might first bag the bag."

They agreed upon a ruse, and, after some chit-chat, talked Mike into its implementation.

"I'll talk with my friend in the CIA."

16

The Man awoke, made his coffee, shaved and showered and scrubbed himself clean, as if in dedication to a new escapade. He saw himself as hero in a picaresque scenario: he would cross magically into the future on stepping-stones made from human skulls. Death would await him and welcome its master worker into a secret aura.

Not being able to discuss his purpose with anyone, and doubting that anyone would listen, he accepted that no one would take *him* "for real." If you said, "Martians are landing in New Hampshire" who would go there? If you said, "Traitors are being guillotined in the Place de la Concorde," they would answer, "Of course, everyone knows that." And some might go, some might not, and *that*, would be, *that!*

The Man reviewed his achievements, and their faculties : his auto, his pistol, a poisoned syringe, and the ferocious tomahawk purchased on a Mexican vacation. The rapier on the wall didn't count. The remaining possibles : a stiletto, a Bowie knife, and a garrote or strangle-cord, both easy to make! He did not want to part with the stiletto, it was of beautiful Italian manufacture and sharp enough to carve roast beef. To strangle was a struggle, but it was quiet. If he selected that means, the next victim would be a female.

He must take no chances!

For a sporting 'event', he might use a snake, a cobra, a coral snake, a…you could get one but they were easily traced through suppliers. He couldn't see himself ensnaring a rattler in the wilds. Moreover, a person could be bitten and call an ambulance. So that was out, even as he enjoyed a vision of himself as Pharaoh, the cobra on his crown, coming suddenly alive and lashing out to bite.

What about a 'blunt instrument'? He'd overlooked that one. However commonplace, it would afford a stint of clobbering and bashing his victim. If he could isolate his quarry, he would have the pleasure of killing him slowly, first by a light blow, then a concussion, then smashing the bone and pulping the cranium. A cudgel, a truncheon, a night stick, a…*lead pipe*. His mind roved back into youth and into the game of *Clue*. He'd overlooked two other possibles, candlestick and the wrench. Both deadly. But fanciful.

He regretted these lists, of victims and that of weapons. What was the term, "anally retentive"? Guess he was. The infinite resource of chance had already served him well. He liked the graceful heft of a lead pipe, but what else…yes…*a golf putter.* That had enormous leverage, that could kill with one blow. It could be wiped off and returned to the bag, put in the trunk, and driven off. Yes, wiped off, *carefully* wiped off. He could use his own putter, kill someone at the club by smashing in his head, then wiping the putter off, put the guilty rag into the golf bag, but *inside the plastic cocaine sac.* The evidence would nicely disappear, and Juan and his customers were not likely to complain.

He also considered that a small lead pipe could be hidden in the golf bag itself, around the handle of the putter. Surely, in one or another of local construction sites, he could find one.

Double trouble! Find a lead pipe, in the rubble!

It was delivery day tomorrow, he weighed out his kilo of coke, placed it into a new tabbed freezer bag, and sealed it tightly. He wanted to rest easy and go right to sleep but could not, lacking a decision as to man or woman as his next pigeon. If it was a wrench or lead pipe, it would have to be a man. Lead pipes first order.

Tomorrow would be a busy day!

17

Harry and Mike both felt stupid asking about a golf bag, and elected Judge, who was at the club several times a week, to do so. Judge Rugh had been Harry's roommate at Yale, and remained at Yale Law, Harry saying "I'll never be lawyer, a licensed scoundrel." Judge said "I agree, but it's fun being a scoundrel, and the money's good."

Judge had still not married, but had helped Harry with his divorce. "Be as dishonest as you like," Harry told him. "Louisa was a wonderful lady, now she's turned hag." Judge loved and admired Louisa French Saybrook, and knew she and Harry still loved each other, but had come undone, two pieces of a puzzle, unfit for the jigsaw mosaic of modern society.

She had not been sent to any of the Seven Sisters, but to Hollins College in Virginia. Her family was old and Southern in the style of Maryland, but had left the growing slum called 'Baltimore' to be near the Capitol, as Louisa's father worked for the State Department. One of their major arguments began when Harry asserted "What the hell *does* the State Department *do,* but *waste money*?" Louisa allowed no one to insult her father, that was that.

Louisa was almost as good at golf as Harry, and often beat Judge when they played a threesome. Judge had settled the details of the divorce on the course, quite amicably, and she had signed the papers at the Nineteenth Hole. "Not under the influence," she printed beneath her signature. Ah, memories! Maybe they'll reunite!

Judge, curious about the golf bag angle already, had bribed several caddies to keep their eyes 'peeled.' A week later he had a sketchy verbal report on three suspicious bags, almost interchangeable, none of which had a name tag but which regularly appeared on the rack. This bag thing was a simple ploy but if the suspect used two, it would be a neat exchange. He would leave one bag, and pick up another similar bag. Why a third? Judge saw no other use for the "bag system" than the delivery of drugs to an unknown party. That party would also be affiliated with the club, the supplier or the seller.

He thought first of the stretch limo, which often arrived at the club with a load of the rich, but the culpable party might be a corrupt member of the club — perish the thought! — maybe the golf pro, whose reputation was spotty. Dave Chick, the carded professional, approached retirement, maybe he needed a cash allowance. Possibly Dave Chick could stuff the bag himself when no one was looking, but that didn't clarify the odd circumstance of the mild mannered mystery man in the parking lot whom Harry had met. That he seemed extraneous caused Judge to take him seriously.

The more Judge thought about it, more possibilities came into his head. It had to be simple if it was to work. He could not dismiss that condition. So, upon locating two of the bags identified by his caddie informants, he carefully opened one side pocket of one and inserted the radio location device Mike had supplied through Harry's CIA pal, "Good Old Roger". Who told Harry a local store where he could buy it.

He phoned Harry. "I've got the receiver with me, and if the signal changes I'll do my best to follow it. But you guys will get stuck with the surveillance, chasing down the fox. I'm a magistrate, don't you know, and cannot be tangled in such a mess."

Harry phoned Mike and they 'made arrangements.'

No one seemed to notice on the following day when the innocuous man came in, left his bag, picked up another and left. However, he had not taken Judge's choice. The telltale golf bag would sit undisturbed for a week. The club's security cameras were ineffective or out of focus, no information there. When Harry and Mike came to check the transmitter, thinking its batteries were dying, they found it in the bag, untampered with and where it had been put.

Nor could they determine which bags on the rack were newly situated. The rack had twenty spots, and another bag vaguely resembled its fraternal twin, so vaguely that at first glance, anyone could have mistaken it, and could have taken it home.

"First week, failure," Mike said. "Batteries OK. Let's leave it for another week and see."

A caddie had been watching them, but Mike had fortuitously designed the transmitter as a transistor radio, which he replaced by considerable sleight of hand. When Harry asked him about the bag exchange, the young man, eager to please, pointed out two more plain examples. "These bags got moved here by Mr. Chick yesterday, they're for the party coming later."

By which he meant that the stretch limo was due on its extravagant errand.

18

Almost seven perfect days of idleness! When the Man unpacked his golf bag with the payment for cocaine, he also took out his putter, and around its base of expensive leather windings (so friendly to the hand) he placed the lead pipe, found at a construction site. He'd cleaned it carefully, and it now cradled the putter without shaking or rattling. He found the pipe clung loosely to the shaft. If he carefully extracted the putter from the bag, the lead pipe would not dislodge itself yet be easily removed.

That would prove very helpful, he was sure!

He was adrift in time. The trombone player had been killed, what, two weeks ago…he had to go to his calendar. He counted the days and stopped, it had nothing to do with the urge. His mission. The Man must claim another…*scalp!* If only he'd had five minutes with the dead trombonist. He would now have an actual scalp, and he would have hung it over his garden box of cannabis! No time for that! Damn you, Fate! What a stupid idea!

Stop thinking and dreaming, just plan your next adventure!

Time was otherwise *not* of the essence: he could murder every day, given space *and* time. Accident had addicted him to mayhem, like an 'instant' alcoholic, baptized by his first drink, or, a compulsive gambler, winner of a lottery, only to be led by his luck into endless future bets, and bankruptcy. Time was, though, *of the quintessence:* he had to claim his mark, kill him or her, wipe off the lead pipe or putter, put the rag into the cocaine sac, deliver the bag on time, and skedaddle!

Now, *that* was *not* thinking *crazy*.

Driving the Cadillac mechanically around town, the Man calmed down. He knew he must stay away from the club, save on deliveries, and the B-Ballers Sports Bar, the environs of MLK and its Negro denizens, the distant park of protestors, and certainly the lane where Beulah Braintree had been shot. He thought of his list and asked himself if fate would send a real estate agent, his instincts cried out for a male target. "Let's go huntin' and fishin'," he thought, "and what the hell?"

The several real estate offices along the boulevard were all posh; the entire area boasted only one RE/MAX. He pulled into the lot of JONATHAN BAXTER REALTY but saw few vehicles there, which was good, the agents were out working. So, no reason to enter its premises and court a roving eye.

His next locale was the glimmering glass headquarters of SUTTON & SIMPSON REAL ESTATE BROKERS. Its parking lot held two Mercedes, one Cadillac, two Lincolns, one Rolls and a Maserati. He thought it must specialize in industrial or commercial properties, but no, not only : he could see residential listings in the front window. There was no movement inside, but the plate glass, opaque and reflective was see-out one way. They were looking at him! No, they were not. He was paranoiazing. They were accustomed to fancy automobiles.

It was already lunchtime and an expensively dressed secretary, or agent, came out the front steps and flashed her fabulous legs. She was intent only on getting into her Lincoln, it turned out, and leaving. A heavy set man in Brooks Brothers clothing came out, huffing and puffing. "You damned bitch!" He shook his fist at the Lincoln but it was too far gone for her to notice, the Man thought. The businessman sat down on a cast iron and mahogany bench, then stamped his foot. "You damned bitch!"

"I hope you don't mean me," said the Man. He had rolled down his window. "I've never been called that before."

The fellow took out his handkerchief and gently wiped his brow. "Sorry. We're very busy and that girl can't be bothered to finish some paperwork. Beauty appointment, damn her." He approached the Man. "Nice, nice, I've never seen a Cadillac so gussied up. What year is it?"

The Man answered quietly, as the fellow leant on his window edge, "I'm looking for a waterfront property in this area. It has to be private, with a swimming pool and Jacuzzi. I will be paying cash, no mortgage headaches. Can you help me?"

The red flush in the realtor's face reduced to a prosperous pink. "You're talking about a million dollar property, and yes, we have several, but you can't see them without proper credentials. I'm Rutherford Bullock, one of the partners here. And you are…?"

The Man answered quietly, "Just call me Charlie." He then gave as reference his lawyer in Boca Raton. Bullock smiled broadly. "I know him by reputation. Did he send you here?"

"More or less. There are two other agencies he also suggested. But, if you're busy, I can come back…"

"You came to the right office," Bullock answered. "I was just going out to lunch, but that can wait. Let's check out the listings from the outside first, then, we can make the appropriate appointments?"

The Man mentioned the lawyers' name again and said, "Phone him and double-check. He handles all my real estate closings. Mind you, I am trying to raise funds also for a condominium in Palm Beach. As he might tell you…"

Rutherford Bullock turned jolly. "We can help you there too! Why don't we have lunch first, on me, of course, and discuss matters at a civilized table, let's say…" He referred to a famous fabulous restaurant with astronomical prices. "What do you say, *Charlie*?"

Inspiration then struck. He saw a simple way to isolate Rutherford Bullock and to quell the greedy sparkle in those pale blue eyes, also predictably bloodshot. "Why don't we have a round of golf first? I'll buy you lunch at my club."

The Man could see Bullock had examined and absorbed every detail of his luxury auto. It still radiated its 'detailing' in Boca Raton. He saw likewise that Bullock was mystified and intimidated. He said, again, softly and in a tease, "What do you say, *Rutherford*?"

"Just call me 'Ruth'. Excuse, but do you have a phone in this buggy? It looks as if you could live in there!"

The Man knew Bullock was trying to josh him, and laughed a subdued chortle. "You're very observant. Why, do you want to make a call?"

Rutherford kept his eyes focused on the Man's own inscrutable, almost Asiatic, glance. "Maybe we should flip for it. How did you know I loved golf?"

"You bear a slight resemblance to Sammy Snead. No, I saw you once on our course. You're a real slammer."

Bullock smirked, remained silent and answered, "Charlie, you're on. But let's just flip a coin. Heads, I buy you lunch, tails, you buy me lunch. We can relax, talk business, and play golf *after* our repast."

"OK, 'Ruth', flip the coin. I'll cover my eyes."

Predictably, Bullock picked up the coin, clenched it in his hand, and said, "Heads it is, I buy you! Do you know how to get to…"

"Yes. Do you want me to drive?"

"Not today. I have a late afternoon appointment here, as we're closing a deal and I must, must, must be there! You can follow me, but as for the golf, we'll be lucky to finish nine holes."

"Rutherford, do you have your clubs in your auto?"

The man nodded with a broad smile. Nice new teeth! "What is your club, Charlie?"

"Tell you what, *Mister* Bullock." Oh, the inspiration, it came simply and tripped off the Man's tongue! "Tell you what, in the interest of time. On the way, we'll be near the Palmgrove Driving Range. We'll stop there, hit a basket or two on the range, and chat, and then we'll visit the restaurant. We can play a full round another time, which, I am sure, we shall!" Mocking the man's speech now he finished: "What do *you* think of *that*?"

"Sounds good. I haven't hit a basket of balls for months. It would build up an appetite."

"Well, it pretty well guarantees that you'll be back here this afternoon, unless we have a Chinese feast."

"God, Charlie, no. No golf course, but the driving range! Let's say a three course lunch, soup, salad, meat and dessert. What do you say to *that*?!"

The Man adjusted his sunglasses. "Doesn't that make *four*?"

The Man had often visited the Palmgrove Driving Range and knew chances were good few people would be there at this hour, and he figured few would take notice of two men in business suits slamming like Sammy Snead. He surmised that Bullock was surely a scratch golfer, he was bulky and strong, and when he rolled back his sleeves later, the Man saw his forearms were thick and sinewy, and that meant a very long ball. The range was set well off the main road, almost in a sandy vacancy, a backroad, under 'future development.' The road to the range was sandy and paved, like many others, with a crunchy layer of sea shells. They drove to the range and parked side by side.

Two middle aged women were finishing their basket of yellow balls, one with exaggerated grace, driving nicely but not far, whereas the other swung her oversized driver to hammer the ball out of sight, yet miffed the stroke. "Goddammit," she said. "I'm never playing this game again. Never!"

"You said that last week, Grace."

"Yeah, I'll repeat myself next week, Josie. I just can't swing like you, it's more like ballet than golf. But when I *connect*..."

Bullock and the Man listened to the bantering, and both smiled. Bullock made a fuss over taking out his clubs and brushing them off. He had a sleek shiny black leather bag, and red and white socks on the woods. "Elegant," said the Man. "That bag is *magnificent*..."

"You won't believe this, Charlie, but that bag is pure Morocco and was given to me by a client...from...Saudi Arabia."

The Man now stalled for time. He wanted the women to leave, which would leave Bullock and himself alone on the range. Perfect timing and time enough? The range had been automatized. One put a dollar in the slot and a basket of balls came out on a clever conveyor. It was impossible to reach inside the door to steal another basket, or 'bucket' as the management called them. The 'bucket' was of heavy mesh coated with delicious yellow plastic. When one finished, one left the 'bucket' in a broad wooden trough.

The Man noticed that a new bill reader had been installed. You could feed a dollar bill, or a five, and you would get the 'bucket' and your change would pour out as quarters into a huge chrome cup, like a public telephone refund.

After some clucking and chit-chat, the women left in a cloud of dust, without saying 'hello' or giving the two gentlemen a second glance. The Man had opened his trunk, but used it to shield his face from the women. Bullock came over holding his driver with the red-and-white stocking.

"Hell, Charlie, that is what I call a trunk. You could live there!"

"Would you like to have a nap inside," said the Man, "I'm going to feed my alligators later."

Bullock laughed loudly and slapped him on his shoulder. "I'll buy the first two buckets. Helluva good idea, Charlie, coming here. But how come you're taking your bag? It's a driving range."

"I need some irons practice, 'Ruth'. I'm not a power hitter like you, so I have to be really good with my irons." He looked around the countryside, it was blank. There was an old tractor in a distant field, and, at the far end of the range, a flock of egrets hunted food.

"Why do you have red and white on your socks, 'Ruth'?"

"Graduate of Cornell. School colors, Charlie. What about you?"

"School of hard knocks, as you'll discover." He knocked his driver and his three wood together. "I can't afford such luxury."

"Luxury, shit," said Bullock. "My wife knitted them." He strode manfully ahead.

The Man was very happy now. He liked to kill people from Cornell. They weren't really Ivy League, in his view. He would take the lovely socks, he knew that also. Must be careful, careful, careful… about prints.

Bullock's first four drives were over three hundred yards, which set the egrets to flight. "Perfect aim," he said. The Man knocked a few with his three wood, so he would have an excuse for shorter distance. He didn't do it badly, almost two hundred yards on one. Over his shoulder he watched Bullock slamming them, one after the other, one shot hitting the 325 marker, they could hear the clang. But he chose to take one iron after the other, and hit two or three finicky balls, then tried another club.

Bullock had exhausted his bucket and flopped back on the bench nearby, loosening his tie and wiping his brow. "Man, that was good Charlie, great idea. I haven't swung so hard for so long! Are you almost through?"

"Not quite."

Bullock tucked the handkerchief into his shirt pocket. Then he reached into his jacket and took out a cigar. "Time for a smoke, Charlie. Man, I feel good! Just a few puffs, OK, and we'll get on to the restaurant?" He lit up.

"Sure, I've only a half dozen balls left."

When the Man took out his putter, Bullock began to laugh. "You are something else, Charlie. A putter on a driving range! What are you, a puttzer?" He regaled himself in smoke and laughter. "Come on!"

The putter was a heavy model and, in a perfect arc, it smacked Bullock's head. He dropped the cigar. "What the fuh…". Then the heavy putter connected again with greater force. Bullock rolled to the ground and tried to get up on all fours.

The Man now unloosed the lead pipe and landed the first blow on Bullock's forehead, then upon the center of his skull. There was a heavy crunch, and again, and again, he swung with both hands. Now the victim's cranium opened and the brains oozed out like spilt porridge. Again, again, the Man struck with the lead pipe, crushing the head, the face, pounding the cerebral pudding into the paving stones. When he could no longer lift the bludgeon, the Man wheezed, almost out of breath, and heard his lungs sigh independently. He coughed up some phlegm and spat it out.

What had been a sculptured, although balding, head was now a variegated eggplant with two pale eyes askew. The Man took out his wipe and cleaned the putter, then put it in his bag. He wiped the pipe free of prints and left it next to a sagging ear. Blood still bubbled from the neck and from the mouth and its grinning teeth. In the distance the egrets, once more hunting for worms and snails, cackled their thanks. The Man hoped they would fly over and feast on Bullock's eyes.

Time, time! He looked at his watch and quickly had the Cornell sock in his hand, but put it in his bag, then trotted to Bullock's car and opened the trunk. He pulled off the other knits and tucked them away. The Man looked around like a fox at dawn, but the back road was quiet, a slight afternoon breeze tickled the trees. He took the incriminating rag and, into the cocaine baggie it went. All so neat, so…fortuitous. So beautiful, and, so barbaric!

As he sought the main road he noticed another car coming, and found a shady thicket that, by a fortuitous curve, concealed him until they passed. Two women as before, but not Grace and Josie. Both yakking to each other, unobservant. The Man thought they might see him in the rear view mirror, he even hoped they would. It would be just more confusing evidence for the Police. Nonetheless, he gave them several minutes to go on to the range.

He had not checked inside Bullock's Mercedes for a telephone, but in following him, Bullock had made no such motions. The fellow's questions suggested he was, however, considering the purchase of one. If Bullock had phoned the lawyer or his office or the restaurant, he, the Man, might be compromised. No worry then. No phone, who knew Bullock's whereabouts?

But how perfect it had been, how fated, how fatal! *"A fat businessman smoking a cigar…"* from His prophetic list. *A real estate agent. Two in one!* Admittedly, the last two on his list, but, additions would be made. Later, he would make them, first, deliver the cocaine.

In the quiet afternoon dropping off the bag at the club was a thirty second chore. He scouted first. No one in the pro shop, caddies out to lunch, no one, except a middle aged fellow finishing an enormous glass of beer on the Nineteenth Hole. A man he had seen before. As the man drank deeply, he came up a shortcut and was gone.

19

Judge Rugh had not seen the Man slip in and out, but after his latest swallow, noted that the stretch limo had arrived. A foursome emerged, two couples. They laughed on their way into the club, and the chauffeur carried two bags from the trunk of the limo to the pro shop rack. That was a courtesy to be expected, but Judge saw the chap pick up another bag from the rack and bring it to the car. It was plain and differed greatly from the bags of the smart set.

Judge immediately went over and introduced himself.

"Nice to meet you, sir," said Juan. He placed the bag near the trunk of the limousine. "Thinking of hiring our service?"

"No, I was thinking you have my bag there."

"I hope not," Juan returned. "This bag belongs to another client. He left it here before but wants to play on another course. Why don't you have a look?"

Judge saw the red and white stocking caps on the woods, and that the bag strongly resembled the others Harry and Mike had checked out, plain pale leather with no brand. He took note of the shiny putter and the variety of pockets. Opening the top one, he found it full of golf balls. But he did not recall ever having seen the socks before on any bag at the club, they signalled something, he knew not what. Such things were old-fashioned, but some people liked them. Be kind to your niblick and mashie! Let your putter shine!

"Here's the man's name and address," Juan offered, taking a card from another compartment in the bag. Judge did not read it entirely — it would have to be bogus — and he did not want to offend 'John Smith.' "You said your name was 'Rugh'" said Juan. "Of course, it's an easy mistake. This bag is nothing special." He chuckled and put his hand on Judge's shoulder. "Neither is Mr. Smith."

He put the bag inside the trunk and slammed shut the lid.

"Sorry," said Judge. "There's been some mischief with bags lately. Dave Chick asked me to keep an eye out, as I'm often here."

Juan smiled graciously. "I am also, Señor Rugh. We have many clients who come here, they often own shares in the club. It's a new club, as I'm sure you know, and they like to check up on their holdings."

"One might steal a bag, but not the golf course," replied Judge. "Have you seen anything in your many trips one might call 'suspicious'?"

"You will appreciate that my services are confidential, I don't spy on my customers. One lady complained that some balls were stolen from her bag, many weeks after the fact. Another gentleman kept expensive cigars in his bag, and they were in fact taken. But so many of those bags were just average, they could easily be carried off by mistake. I keep telling my people to put large name tags on them, but they seem to think it's an invasion of privacy. I just drive them around and say, 'Yes, sir' 'No, sir' 'Yes, ma'am'…"

"I gotcha," said Judge. "Do you take people to the airport?"

"Of course!" Juan answered. "My major base of operations. Most of my business! Arranged, of course, in advance."

"How much do you charge?"

Juan gave Judge his card. "When you need a limousine, call us, Señor Rugh, and we'll quote you."

Judge said, "Thanks for helping. One can't be too careful. I guess you know the club has installed some fancy security cameras."

Juan raised his eyebrows slightly. "It's happening everywhere. That's nice to know. But I don't really care. All I require is a bit of shade and a quiet afternoon when I take a nap inside the car. Wait *on* the customers, wait *for* the customers! If there's any valuables inside, I even crank back a seat and sleep there overnight."

"Lots of room within!"

"Indeed, Señor Rugh. Take a look. We can comfortably transport ten people."

Judge smiled. "That's nice to know… too."

He wondered if his idea about the location beacon would ever work. It had stayed in place for almost an extra week. As for the 'wily Juan' Judge could form no conclusion, except general distaste.

He returned to the Nineteenth Hole and found Harry and Mike waiting for him at his table.

20

"While you were guzzling," Mike shot out, "our killer, we presume, was bashing in a fellow golfer's head."

Judge had ordered a late lunch which the waiter whirled into place. "Enjoy," he said, effeminately.

"Better eat first," said Harry. "This is one corpse no one will want to examine closely. Complete pulping of the head, brains splashed on the soil…"

"OK, Harry," said Judge. "Try not to be explicit."

They related the time frame, and Judge returned a quizzical look. He verbally reviewed — between visible mouthfuls of a Reuben sandwich — what he had learned from the chauffeur. That the caddies had seen nothing. The stretch limo was back. Bags were bags.

It was a slow, hot day, no one on the tee for two hours. "I was just luxuriating in the sun, listening to this receiver, which has been a model of monotony. Unless they're using just one bag, hither and yon, we have to catch on because when they use the baited bag, it will at least signal to whom the bag belongs. We can then track it around town, and analyze the travel. We look, *then* we leap."

Mike nodded, thanking Judge for the beer he'd unknowingly just purchased. Harry lifted his glass. He said, "You say you inspected the bag and it belonged to a 'John Smith.' You were being 'had'!"

"I *had* no choice," said Judge. "I pretended the bag was mine, but didn't notice at first the unusual wool socks on the drivers. That still rings a bell. I once played golf with a big fellow whose wife used to make socks for golfers, for their clubs, that is, not their feet."

"Does the name 'Rutherford Bullock' ring the bell louder?"

"Yes!" said Judge, putting down his sandwich. "I know him, he's big in real estate and a fairly good on the links. Longest drive in this area. I would say he averages three hundred yards, a few more than our friend Harry here."

Harry rebuked him with a grimace.

"Maybe we *are* getting somewhere," Mike mused. "Let's assume those stockings came from the bag of Rutherford Bullock, who died about two hours ago. He was found at the Palmgrove Driving Range, which is only ten minutes from here. That might argue that the killer stole the socks from Bullock after killing him, and made a beeline right here."

Harry interposed, "To display his successful homicide?"

Judge finished the Reuben and wiped his mouth as usual. "My bad luck, because I was eating or drinking when he came, as the bag was there half an hour ago, at least, for the stretch limo had just rolled in. But it's awfully close timing."

"It will be our bad luck to discover Mrs. Bullock was prolific in her knitting habits. You can't buy hosiery for clubs anymore. But we don't know when the bag got put on the bench, unless it was very recently but it could have been last night. One assumes that Bullock had the same stockings on hand when he was killed." Mike drank, then tapped the table. "Someone tell me how the golf bag and the murders are connected."

Judge waved at the waiter and ordered another round. "Certainly that's obvious. The golf bags are a way to communicate, and probably there is a drug ring in operation. One party brings a bag full of heroin or cocaine, and probably receives payment in another. This may relate to the murders, as some club member may know about the arrangement. Or, it's part of the limousine business."

Mike nodded. "Too many loose pieces. Let's go back to the murders. Drugs we can stop one way or another. Or pass them off to the Feds. Harry?"

Harry adjusted his sunglasses. "We know the time of death almost to the minute. Forensics phoned us just before we got here. The body was found by two women who arrived and found Bullock dead, his blood still wet, un-coagulated. However, they saw no one there, just the victim's car. One lady thought she saw a car driving away, but can't remember it, or, may have imagined it.

Forensics says the tire tracks are similar to previous examinations, so it might be the same killer."

Mike said, "Might makes right! Fooey. I'm going to check the parking lot right now, we might luck out." But he returned frowning. "Too damn many tracks, some delivery trucks and that stretch limo, parking here and there, ending up in its usual perch."

"Still," Judge said, "even a minor trace, that would be something."

"You can park, leave your car running, carry a bag in the back way, a shortcut alongside the rack, and be gone in a minute. If no one saw a thing, *that*'s probably what happened."

"If it was the Milquetoast with his custom built Caddie," said Harry, "he would certainly avoid detection in either case. I sense a weasel. Quick up the walkway, turn right to the pro club, or take the shortcut, keep a sharp eye, drop the bag, and then, tootle off. Perhaps with another bag. No one is going to arrest him, he can say the bag is his own, or he was carrying it up but changed his mind. We don't know who he is, whether he's even a member here, and as the club is intensely private, it won't be easy to find out, even for Judge."

"I think I can handle all the details," Judge said. "Proceed."

"Bad news first," Mike muttered. "Bullock had a disagreement with a woman in his office, who flipped him the bird and went to lunch. They had a big deal closing that afternoon and she was derelict in paperwork. She seemed to recall a car pulling in just as she left, but her recollection is…*nil*. One hour later Bullock was bludgeoned to death with a lead pipe. I mean totally clobbered. The pipe showed no sign of prints, and was found next to Bullock's splattered head. We can't tell if the cigar, found doused in his blood, was Bullock's or the perp's. There is no cashier at the range, it's pay cash through the window and the balls come out. Very automatic, very anonymous. Which suggests to me that Bullock was lured there as part of the murder plan. May have something to do with the big real estate deal the secretary told me about. But the killer could obviously have taken out Bullock in another way." He paused to drink. "The use of a cudgel suggests that he held some grudge against Bullock, perhaps he took his golf club stockings as a trophy…petty revenge."

Judge spoke. "Perhaps. He was a big man, this Rutherford. They called him 'Ruth' pronounced like 'Rough.' Does this not suggest the killer was also big, strong, and knew Bullock, perhaps through business?"

"The autopsy will be done tonight," Mike answered, "we're just speculating. A small man could have shot him, whatever, then pulped away the evidence. Struggle or no struggle. I had one case where a guy's head was turned to jelly just to extract the bullet what done him in."

"*Was* there a struggle?" asked Harry.

"Apparently a *slight* one. Bullock had been struck down, his hands and knees were well-dusted, but he flopped over on his back and the killer pounded him to mush with the lead pipe, and that was a hefty lead pipe too. Of ancient vintage."

Mike admitted that the report was fresh and incomplete, they would have to review the autopsy, and see what else forensics discovered. "Just give me one valuable tidbit," he prayed, hands together, raised to Heaven.

The afternoon had cooled slightly, and the two couples were on the first tee. They were young, in their early thirties, and on vacation, Harry thought. Full of themselves. Much in love. Ready to tee off on their own amorous course!

As he and Louisa once had been!

21

The Man was exultant as he sat in the Turkish
bath, inhaling steam and perspiring a fine sheen.
Exhaustion came slowly but his vigor was reborn in a cold
shower. "To close my pores, to close my pores…" but he
found he had become erect. The icy flow subdued this
ornament, and he exited in a fleecy towel, soft as a moth's
cocoon. He dried himself quickly, lay down on a cot and
slept.

'Yet another baptism', he dreamt.

As he dried and dressed himself later he imagined a
way to camouflage his dealings: he would buy shares in a
funeral home. Then more enjoyment would ensue from
the rituals of interment or cremation. He had once visited
a crematory and knew the ovens each had a fireproof
porthole so workers could supervise the decomposition.
Everyone took a different time from flesh to ashes. Then,
into the bone grinder. He would revel in the process, a
voyeur, or vicarious necrophile. The Police could not

photograph that, because, as he knew, with serial killings, they often took shots of all funereal mourners. Not a portrait he coveted!

At his apartment he ordered a late night pizza with 'the works'. Its tomato sauce, onions, sausage, pepperoni, peppers and anchovies brought back Rutherford Bullock's facial potpourri. He had asked for extra sauce and no cheese, so producing the effect of a blood pie. "I brought ya some parmesan in this cup," said the delivery boy, "just so you got *some* cheese." *Here's your big tip, sonny!*

Now, two mushrooms from his refrigerator were set as eyes on the pizza. He tore it apart hungrily and ate large bites. The sauce was hot, and he knew the roof of his mouth would be burnt, but picking off strands of dental tissue on the morrow suited his fancy. O, 'twas flesh and blood that kept life going!

The next morning it was time to think again what type of a serial killer he should become. Like choosing what kind of lawyer you wanted to be, a probate lawyer, a defense attorney, a corporate honcho, a…well, you had to make a choice. Something special, better, something unique.

One thing impossible, to cannibalize, like some infamous slayers, who collected trophies, except for the golf socks, that disgusted him. Nor did he plan on sending ears or fingers to the bereaved. He wanted an artistic plan, with a touch of glory, a Sistine Chapel of many panels. Murder must not kill sleep. No MacBeth, no witches. The pace to tomorrow and tomorrow must not be petty, but profane.

He laid gingerly back on his bed, and before a morning nap, felt like a soldier back from the wars. When the noontide came, he would know. He would see many miles down the road ahead.

The morning newspaper delighted him with its exposition taking half the front page. Rutherford had been famed for being a "developer" and a "golf wizard." In fact, the Man had known something of his victim beforehand, simple data, but nothing of his appearance.

The excitement of dispatching him occluded the man's resumé. He read and re-read the obituary near the back, almost a full column. In death, Bullock had robbed five other departed of their proper elegiac space.

The main article, about the murder itself, had allowed the reporter to speculate: it *could* be the work of the "serial killer" known to be at large! Yet it said nothing more about that villain. It did not mention that *his* murders had begun a month ago, and that *he* projected a future of years. If you're going to predict, go whole hog!

Some crazy coot, he recalled, on a back road in Kentucky had killed thirty some people before being caught. He'd butchered them and fed the pieces to his hogs. The skulls he kept in a cabinet, in a neat row, a smiling chorus. Otherwise no accurate count could have been made. Time to fashion his own approach *something* like that. Did he really need it? Of course not! He had a genius for murder! There was quantity, there was quality. One might fantasize, to what effect?

Leisure time today, what to do? He decided on a round of golf.

"We ought to start a breakfast club," Mike groused.

"What about a prayer-breakfast, like the politicians have?" Harry smiled to himself. "What do they do at such meals? When I heard that Lyndon Johnson gave such, I could hardly stop laughing. That unholy crook!"

"Rest in peace, Harry. You'll love Medicare, and the Great Society. It's still too soon to judge him." Mike, you damned Liberal!

"Let's stick to the menu. Summon the wench with *la décolleté*." Harry was angered by Mike's remark, he despised anything that connoted welfare or Medicare or socialism. And, he was possessive of Giselle's bosom. The progress of the investigation irked him severely. He was glad the restaurant could not supply Mike with his bowl of Cheerios.

"I'm sorry, sir, but Giselle isn't working today."

"And you are?"

The waitress was slim and younger than her colleague. "I'm Lucy. You know, sir, I think she really likes you."

"How gratifying," Mike put in. He had the good looks of George Segal, but Harry outshone him, blonde and blue-eyed like the young Peter O'Toole.

"Send her my love!" Harry said. "And bring us…"

The order was given and delivered five minutes later. "How can they cook the bacon so fast?" Mike asked. "And why don't they have Cheerios?"

Harry knew the 'chef' and explained that in breakfast nooks bacon was cooked in large ovens, and then heated up on the grille. He looked at his plate and missed Giselle. She always gave him an extra piece.

"The final forensics." Mike handed him the report. He read it twice and returned the slim dossier. "Those two women *would* have to park right over where the murderer parked. These other tire marks, just cheap stuff, it says, like they put on Ford Escorts. There was another car there before Bullock's, and let's hope those people come forth. We have smudges, no prints, we have slight footprints on sea shells and we have a *possibility* that *two* blunt instruments were used…"

"There's no question about the lead pipe, it was full of blood and brain tissue. The edge of the pipe could have inflicted those small lesions, but it hardly matters. Just tell me how a big guy like that didn't see the lead pipe coming at him." Harry picked up his bacon and devoured it, inch by inch. "Was there another killer who came along?"

"No, we know there were two buckets of golf balls served, and one was exhausted. The other was left near Bullock. If the killer had a golf bag, and don't those damn things keep popping up, he could have kept the pipe inside the bag."

"He had established a rapport with Bullock, probably pretended to take out a club and bashed him unawares. The first blow didn't knock Bullock out, he fell down on all fours and then the next blows totalled him."

Harry agreed. "He was duped into visiting the range, so the killer knew how the range worked and its schedule. It's busy on the weekend, but not during lunch hours on working days. That's when I'd go there."

"My guess, the killer waited for Bullock to light his cigar. Can't imagine him lighting the cigar and pulling out the lead pipe. Those pipes are easily found on many construction sites in this area, as they're being replaced by PVC."

"Mike, ever play *Clue*? You've got the gun, the rope, the knife, the lead pipe, the…"

"Yeah, I know. But no automobile, no candlestick, and no doggone tomahawk. I don't think our killer is playing any kind of game. He is a natural. He is lucky. And, he will kill again soon."

22

The Man sat at his desk and took out the list he made previously. It had six categories, and in his last jaunt, he had killed a (male) real estate agent, who was also a "fat businessman smoking a cigar." Rutherford Bullock was in fact only pudgy, but big and muscular. He knew he must continually use guile to avoid being killed by the brute himself. With his first slash of the putter hatred had boiled over. He had, in a frenzy, with both hands and all his strength, pounded the broker's head into buzzard bait.

His next victim must fall to the rope or the garrotte. So, carry both. Despite his artfulness, his clothing, an excellent suit, was superficially cleaned and put into a Salvation Army box. His shoes into a Goodwill slot, and his shirt into a YMCA Thrift Store receptacle. Bullock's blood and spillover from the brainpan had not sullied his adventure, but he was disgusted to find how messy his

joyous pastime was becoming. When he found the extent
of the splatter he almost puked, it was like being served
steak on a place mat that pictured a steer in the
slaughterhouse. Splatters were very dangerous evidence
too! Loved by juries! Blood patterns, presented in grisly
scientific exactitude.

The Man pondered his luck. Was there such a
thing? The *fortune of others* had turned bad, and his own
happenstance had been more than happy, it was blessed. If
he encountered misfortune, his career might end, like a
stockbroker's, whose investments came to nothing
overnight. For the moment, his lust sated, he thought to go
another month until his laurels shriveled brown. The urge
for murder would return, he loved its arbitrary sway. But
it knew no timetable.

It was now time to nap, just a little more. Then
he'd play a late nine holes at the club. He fell asleep with
the savor of his crimes, the first insane dispatch of dog
and woman, then the impulsive slaying of the Larry Bird
fanatic, the execution of a worthless Negro, the hapless
Alf, and, a bloated businessman-realtor "smoking a cigar."

Judge Rugh, back at his post decided only one beer, only one sandwich, and no fries, no dessert. He'd bypassed breakfast and slept in, now, sentient and comfortable, he took up the job as sentinel. The receiver always came to life with a beep, so he switched off the sound and relied upon the little flashing red light. Its even pulse assured him that reckoning with the mysterious bagman was imminent. So he hoped. Or else, this experiment should change.

As he was lulled by its rhythm whilst eating his lunch, he failed to notice the Man who materialized at the Pro Shop and who picked up, at last, the baited golf bag. He proceeded to the tee and hit his first shot, then mounted his golf cart and drove off. The receiver was not so sensitive as to note a nearby change, only at distances of several hundred yards. Then, the pulse and beeping slackened. If used in surveillance, therefore, the receiver would respond to an approach from a weaker signal. Its maximum reaction was within a few hundred yards, though it could register, simply via direction, the broadcast unit three or four miles away, faintly, so the stalker had only to point the receiver, follow its direction and watch the red light flicker meaningfully.

Judge had, of course, seen the man approach the tee, hit his shot, and leave, but the bag did not catch his eye, it was nondescript. He knew, up close, differences in the bags they had examined, but not at this distance, and the bag had been laid in the rear of the cart, somewhat circumspect. Judge had never seen the Man before, as had Harry. And, being Judge Rugh, set comfortably in place, he had no urge to leave his perch and visit the parking lot. The receiver told him nothing new: the signal was strong, and did not weaken until the Man reached the fourth green. Half an hour had passed, and Judge was unsure if the signal was attenuating or if the batteries were run down. How could one tell? As in fishing, was the bait being nibbled, or swallowed? One's first surveillance, he thought, must be fraught with flickering lacunae.

He called Harry about the change. "I'll be there," was the reply. That would take another half hour, Judge estimated. Keeping an eye on the approach, and seeing neither Harry nor the stretch limo, his other focus, he ordered another drink. Now, the signal strengthened, as if the bag was coming back. It was stronger when Harry arrived but suddenly went out.

"Well?" asked Harry.

"I think we have a dead duck. The signal was strong, started to fade, then grew strong again. As you got here, it stopped."

Harry laughed. "Blame me!"

The Man had also stopped. He had tired and drove his golf cart to the parking lot. The bag went into the trunk and he closed it. He left the cart beside the Pro Shop and noticed Judge Rugh, now an uncomfortably familiar person, at his usual table, fussing with a portable radio. He instinctively went down the side path and got into his car. The exit road was one-way and looped back into the main entry half a mile down.

Had Harry arrived five minutes earlier, he would have seen the great chromed Cadillac departing. But as Harry parked, the Caddie rejoined the road that led out, past the palms, the crossroads, the fairways, into the posh neighborhoods.

The Man knew not that he carried a telltale bag. He also did not know the heavy steel lid reinforcements, at this distance, virtually blanked its signals. He had felt a false alarm on seeing Judge. That was a spot of panic because he was drained by his exertions, his steam bath, and his renascent desire to murder again.

Panic preyed on pathos.

Tomorrow, he would be ready. Or, the next day. Frazzled, he cared not. As a killer he was ultimately entitled to keep a banker's hours.

23

"We can't go on meeting like this, sweetie," Harry said to Judge, tweaking his nose at the same time.

His friend shook the receiver and heard no rattle. "Seems fine. Sometimes one battery can get off keel and it stops, one bump later, it starts."

Harry opened the device, checked it, and handed it back to Judge. "It's fine. There's possibly some quirk with the transmitter, perhaps its 'directionality', whatever they call it."

"I thought it would be like the James Bond thing when I got it. Probably more CIA castoffs, junk they don't use…"

"What would we do without our friend Roger Lye in Langley? Or our beloved Michael of the Dublin ghetto?"

Judge retold the signal tracing, the initial weakening, then strengthening, then the sudden shut off. He gave times, approximate, but Harry suggested that if he did see someone tee off during that interval, it could well be their suspect. For drug pushing, anyway. But the golf bags formed a chain in his mind. Leave one, with cocaine, take one empty, leave a third to distract or to be checked, if suspicion arose.

Judge's interview with the chauffeur Juan partially solidified this theory. Juan could easily market or subdivide a large shipment of whatever drug arrived. In the case of the murdered pimp, cocaine had been found in his possession and in the needle inside his left forearm. Death came from cyanide, though, it made Harry think. A deceptive killer, one with *panache*. The trombone player Alf had a pocketful of marijuana, yet, sources said he was anti-drugs, so the killer may have wished to incriminate him, with this reddest of herrings.

Spurious minutiae!

"Have you investigated the memberships, and perhaps found the man who drives the refurbished Cadillac?"

Judge shook his head. "I was going to have Mike step in, and with my magisterial authority, imply we could issue a warrant whenever. However, that putative club member might be a John Doe or a John Smith. He could be hiding behind a lawyer or offshore account. As a new club, we weren't too fussy about anything but net worth. So, if he's some rich so-and-so he may be a degenerate with aught else to do but rob banks, sell dope, and murder people."

"I'm going to check the bags and see what's there." When Harry returned he was succinct. "Just one bag, of the three. Plain old bugger."

"That could mean our friend the Mystery Man took one home, Juan the chauffeur has the other, and that leaves the one you just visited. Odd man out. What do you figure, wouldn't this system work very well for the delivery of cocaine or heroin, and the subsequent payment for it?"

Harry smiled. "Nice and neat. Who's going to open golf bags searching for money or drugs? Maybe to steal golf balls, but I bet they are in the accessible top pocket."

"They were," Judge confirmed, referring to his chat with Juan. "Next we'll imagine a golf ball that pops open like an egg to disgorge its opiates. Give them credit, they have a smooth business going, if that's how they run it. The limo connects with rich clientele, that clientele ask for 'recreational drugs' or hookers or, I wouldn't be surprised, well-endowed gigolos."

"We'd be qualified, then, to start up competition." Harry's joke fell flat. Judge disliked any reference to human privates or gross immorality. On the bench, he had it regularly, whores and pimps and dope pushers and blackmailers, black males, white males, and virulent transvestites. He had asked for a transfer to probate, better to die of boredom than disgust.

"We can't have you sitting here all day, three hours each afternoon has barely sufficed. Our 'golfer' is not a morning person. All the murders took place in the afternoon or evening. The first he did not choose but, let's say, it engendered his killer's lust. The second was doubtless impromptu, yet executed with talent. The third a clever masterpiece of seduction, if 'Famous Amos' street wisdom amounted to anything. As for the fourth, well…"

"You still can't link them together," said Judge, "not yet. Maybe the first and second, even the third. The fourth was out of bounds, forty miles away, and the fifth, deliberate but…". He ordered another beer. "Something sticks in my craw, something I've seen, but can't recall."

"It will come to you."

"It's something about golf. That man I saw yesterday, who arrived on the tee and was off in the cart. He disappeared about the time you showed up. At least the caddie told me they found his cart parked near the Pro Shop, after what must have been a brief round."

Harry was tired of beers at the Nineteenth Hole. He requested Campari. "What's that?" The effeminate waiter seemed upset. "I thought we had everything."

"Make it a vermouth on the rocks," Harry replied. "You must have that!"

"Yes, sir, we do!" He danced off. When the drink arrived Harry saw it was doubled in size and with a surfeit of ice cubes, in the shape of tiny golf balls, made in a special machine.

24

Two days passed. The Man came early to the club and left his bag with the beeper to exchange it for a bag replaced by Juan, the bag with the red and white socks, and full of cash. He took the bag to his car and left in the usual manner. He knew it was the caddies' morning for free rounds, and that Dave Chick never showed up before noon. So, once more, he achieved invisibility.

He did not feel like driving to Boca to make his "deposit" so he took out his usual cut, and wrapped the funds in aluminum foil, then in cloth, the first to avoid X-rays and the second to cushion the cargo. He inserted the packet into a bubble envelope and sent it, by certified mail, at the Post Office.

That was all quickly done. Time to enjoy the stockings on the woods and luxuriate in their color and design. The wool was ticklish and sweet against his cheek. He loved the dark red threads. They could be

Cornell, they could also be Harvard. The Crimson. A contrast which made him laugh. Then, he put them in the top drawer of his desk.

Soft and wooly, indeed, he now felt the urge to kill, to kill something soft and wooly, like…a woman? It was like smoking a cigarette. You mightn't be in the mood, but when you saw Humphrey Bogart light up, then you wanted a cigarette. To be a glamorous smoker, or not to be, just inhale and feel the acrid flavor bite into your lungs. A friend had told him rightly, "I love breathing free fresh air, but I also enjoy smoking a cigarette when I drink coffee."

The Man took up his list, written with a careful nib, and chuckled. At some point, Number Four, he would kill a policeman, eating fried chicken or in self-defence. It would come to that some day, then the cops would corner him, like John Wilkes Booth, in a rustic barn. He would not die in the flames, he would come out firing. He would kill at least one more policeman before the crusaders shot him! The Man laughed at his own conceit. He knew he was being foolish, that the wings of imagination needed footsteps first.

He resolved, instinctively, to visit the glories of Death on a woman, this time she must be a middle-aged woman, past her prime, a proud wooly woman, perhaps even a 'liberated' woman, or a stalwart Lesbian marching for 'equality.' Maybe, with hairy legs!

This thought had been deep inside him for years. These women he found to be mostly ugly,, and lacking attention, drew it on themselves via despising men. Somewhere in his collectibles he had a postcard from 1890 of a suffragette. The Victorian artist had framed the Plain Jane with "Do You Want this Woman to Vote?" Ugly women *must* bring ugly politics, we all know that. Ugly women haunted the ruins of Rome!

One condition! He had to be sure the woman marked out was ugly inside and out. She could not be a coarse undesirable like his second victim, she must be a bit regal. She must be taken with the rope or the garrotte, whichever served, to muffle her dispatch. How women could scream! But there was no guarantee. And, he was verging into fields of fussiness.

He *could* fill another syringe with cyanide and bump into her and down she would go. No, that was unsporting. He remembered his vial of morphine, searched his refrigerator, and, found it next to some grated cheese.

Now, *Cherchez la femme*! If that was what was to be. Easy to think of the profile but how to direct one's steps? He knew there were two Lesbian bars on the strip, because he went into one by mistake last year. Besides the general consternation when he entered, he was confronted by a tall athletic female in a leather jacket. Her hair was greased back and she spoke in a deep baritone. "Whaddaya want, sonny?"

Realizing his mistake, he replied, "Is there a public telephone here?"

"Not for you, sonny!"

A petite ingénue dressed in pink, sitting next to a heavy set woman with giant apple-cheeks and a porcine nose, shouted, in most dulcet tones, "Throw him out Babe!"

He recalled the name of the place was BABE'S BABES. "Are you the owner?"

"That's right, sonny. Phone is in the back, and be quick about it."

He deferred to her, almost with a bow. "*Really*, I wanted to use the *men's* room…"

The entire coterie at the bar burst into giggles and chortles. "Sonny, you gotta be kidding!"

He pretended great discomfort. "Are you girls all…*Lesbians*?"

Another slight chorus of laughter. He backed up slowly, as Babe was making a fist and rubbing it. "You know," he said, "I'm a male Lesbian. I'm gay for women!" The bar was deadly quiet. The little demoiselle made a face.

Babe came closer. "You'd better leave, sonny, while you still got two balls."

He wanted to say "Two more than you" but demurred. He did apologize with a wave of his hand. "I don't want to fight," he said to Babe. "Because I know, *I could **lick** anybody here.*"

The bar erupted with screams. His exit was rapid and he nearly collided with two women in leather jackets who had just parked their motorcycles. One raised her fist at him, the other watched. "Sorry," he offered. "There's some bad blood in there."

"Yeah?"

"Yeah," he agreed. "It's Babe. I think she's on the rag."

No one followed him to his Cadillac, and he rejoiced. Women like that, even after a year, could remember and identify him. They were a congregation of spiders. But if he killed Babe, and, however much he wanted to, someone would finger him later. He was sure someone else would kill Babe, as the love of Lesbia was habitually vicious.

He once had a homosexual acquaintance who kept trying to seduce him, only to be murdered by his obsessive lover. The man was found with penis and testicles inside his mouth. Lesbian murders, he was told, often involved intricate and similarly imaginative mutilations.

He thought back, now, fearfully, that if he garrotted Babe, she would shake it off and strangle him! What he wanted was a gentle, loving dykey with a maternal streak. A turtle dove that would alight on his shoulder. A pigeon looking for grain. But he would not find his bird in a barroom. He could not revisit BABE'S. It had gone under six months since.

Now the Man enjoyed the mid afternoon on a cool day, and, without firm intent, he drove to a park near the ocean where he could hear children shouting and watch mothers with prams. Not the neighborhood for his quarry, but a peaceful spot, a stopover, though he felt lucky. He proceeded to a bench and read the newspaper he found on it. Ah, a new article on the "Serial Killer". Nearby, the children, laughing or shouting, were merry birds in a roost.

A young matron with a friendly face approached with her infant in a carriage. He put down the newspaper and shook his head. "I can't believe all these murders lately. One every day!"

The woman stopped and smiled. "It is horrible," she said. "My husband says they'll catch him. He ought to know, he's a cop."   "Does he think all these murders are being done by one person?"

"Some cops do, some don't. Apparently there are several killers, or, if it's just one, he must be very smart."

He nodded, smiled and looked at the carriage but the baby was covered in mosquito netting, or the like. "How old is your baby?"

"Young Josh is six months. We're so proud of him. But please talk quietly, he just went to sleep."

"How fortunate you are. My son is almost a year old, but I haven't seen him for six months. My wife just took off with him. She joined some group of activists, Planned Parenthood or Women's This or That…I've traced her to this area." The woman was obviously empathizing, so he lowered his face, even more histrionically. "You can't imagine what it's like to lose your son!"

He hung his head further, folded the newspaper and slapped the bench. "The police have been no help at all."

"I'm so sorry, sir. There are *so* many runaways. Don't you know more than that? Not much to go on."

He shook his head and faked some tears. "You have no idea…no idea…"

Josh began to fuss in the pram. The woman waited, then relaxed. "It might not be much help, sir, but there's some 'Ladies Freedom' meeting here later. She might come there if she joined that group. Did you see the poster?"

"Thank you, and God bless," he replied. "I'm going now. You've given me new hope." He got up and walked sullenly away. A policeman's wife! Not at all suspicious of him. Was it his own mild manners, his mimicry, or, the infant? That's what a baby will do!

He *had* seen posters up and had read none. The first one he saw satisfied him. There would be a meeting at six p.m. No admission fee. Please come with a donation. Will you help us? "Women everywhere are uniting for the Cause." He looked at his watch. Not long to wait. The Man knew, gleefully, he would be there.

The gathering was unisexual, almost as many men there as women. He had retained the newspaper, and had returned at dusk. One vinegary old gal marched in, leading four young maidens. Another hippy-dippy Hausfrau carried a pair of twins. One statuesque blonde in blue jeans came by sporting her obvious tattoo. For a moment he thought of Jed and Trudy, and a shiver rolled through his abdomen. It wasn't Trudy but, it could have been her sister. Most of the men seemed in tow, wearing a wimpish expression and, all were well beyond uxorious.

Most people passed him by, but, as it darkened, a twosome asked, "May we sit with you on this bench?"

He nodded. One of the women, twice the size of the other, was mustached and glum. The dainty lady with her had an immaculate coiffeur and wore sparkling earrings. Her voice was full of honey, her eyes warm and kind. "I don't think we've met."

"Just call me 'Charlie'. I support this organization financially. They're doing great things. Every now and then I stop by."

"My name is Glenda. Charlie…what?"

"No offence, Glenda but I remain anonymous at these events. If you give money, people find out and solicit you later. You understand, I'm sure."

"Yes, Mr. Charlie but I didn't think our group solicited *big* donations. But I'm not on the board." She moved closer to him. "This is my boyfriend Rex."

The larger woman said nothing but got up, pushed Glenda to his right, and shook the Man's hand with a grip that had either milked many cows or had forced many hockey pucks into the net. "Hi."

"Come to these meetings often?"

Rex looked him over and nodded.
"Glenda makes me. I like to get out, to parks and marinas, outdoors, but she says I'm a natural born couch potato." Rex kept her serious mien.

It was autumn and Daylight Savings Time, now dark, and the park lights came on, distantly. They sat on the periphery, out of view, but with passersby every minute, gradually decreasing in number. The meeting started with a gong, and people settled down. The peaceful air was broken by some faint march music, people rose and sang an anthem, and the speaker approached the microphone to give a prayer. The tall woman on the podium was dressed like a Druid priestess. The Man thought of Bellini's opera, its music. He also thought, "ridiculous."

Was there feedback in the system, a whine? No, it was mosquitoes *en masse*. People all around took up swatting and swaying. Rex lifted her arm and tried to shoo the tropical clouds of insects away. The Man handed her his paper. "Hope that helps."

When she took the paper he stuck the needle filled with morphine in her arm, quickly, like a sniper shooting. "Ouch!" she said. "Jesus, these bugs must be huge!"

The Man slapped his own face as he pocketed the syringe. "Damn right!" Inside his jacket he felt the rope and the garrotte. The pistol, in its holster, remained on his left hip. The stiletto he had stored in a sheath like pocket.

Rex examined her arm. "Damn, how can a bug draw blood?" Glenda leaned over, and gave Rex a kiss. "Mommy will fix it later, hon."

"It could have been a yellow-jacket," the Man offered. "They come out at dusk."

"I don't think so," said Glenda. "I have a garden where they come all day, along with bees, but at sundown we have mosquitoes, and fireflies."

The morphine began its effect. After a few minutes, Rex's head slumped over, bit by bit. "Tired..." she said. "Gotta sleep."

"Honey, are you OK?" Glenda mewed.

"Here," said the Man, "let me help." He got up, got behind them, and slipped the wire garrotte on Glenda's neck. He pulled hard, hard enough, he thought, to amputate her head. He kept pulling and felt her finally go limp. He was livid with excitement. Leaving the garrotte in place, he put the rope around Rex and tightened it. Rex made a slight gurgle. The Man stood in place and kept the noose rigidly in force. When it slackened momentarily he wound the rope around his hand and pulled again. He leaned against the tension and clenched his fist. After an indeterminate pause he knew Rex was no longer breathing. Rex had 'expired'.

It was full night, inky black with a million stars overhead. The harvest moon gleamed, but was obscured by park greenery. The Man looked around and saw with relief that no one was near, and that people in the next row were listening to the address. The mosquitoes remained visible against the park lights, but, as it had grown cold, they began to dissipate. He took the newspaper and left on cat feet.

He was Death riding another's last breath, he was the bird of prey on the rocky mountain apex, flying there...on the silent wings of an owl!

The Man had left the weapons behind, around their necks. This was his first double, two birds with one...well, he'd gotten his wooly woman and the fluff beside her. If only it hadn't been so quick, so painfully *personal!* Strangulation could be the most intimate means to murder, though. The Man could barely credit his own derring-do. He had felt comfortable killing Rex and Glenda, they were a happy couple.

Now, they were dead.

25

Breakfast again, this time with Judge and Mike. Harry signaled for coffee, and was not displeased to see Giselle. She was more voluptuous than ever, cleavage bursting with amour, as she leaned over to pour the cream into his cup. "I've missed you Mr. Saybrook."

"You say that to all the regulars, I bet."

Judge, fascinated by her charms, could not take his gaze away. He tapped his coffee cup and Mike smiled, knowing Giselle would ignore the judge, which she did, unwittingly.

"Coffee!" he insisted.

"Yes, sir." She was miffed, Harry could see, and raised his eyebrows as he regarded Mike.

"She's not a robot, Judge," Mike put in. Giselle was now self-conscious and served Judge with a brusque gracefulness.

"Are you a judge, sir?"

Judge explained, flushing slightly at the attention. He ordered, as did Mike and Harry. "My ticket today," he said.

Giselle stood by, trying to make a decision, then she spoke. "Judge, can you help me then? My brother's in jail, and they won't let him out." She gave the information and Judge nodded.

"I'll see what I can do."

What he would do, Harry surmised, was nothing, and, in avoidance of his duty, Judge would not come to breakfast here for several months.

"I think we may have our man," Mike said. "Last night another murder — at the Terra Ceia Park. Big lezzy named Rex Booker, strangled with a rope. Girlfriend next to her, Glenda Wentworth, was garrotted, but she fainted and the killer assumed he'd killed her. She's doing okay but is still in shock. We can talk to her this afternoon."

"Huzzah," Harry offered. "About time. It could be linked to the other park killing of the trombone fellow?"

"After dark, in the park, meet me there, but beware…" Judge drank his coffee in several gulps. "A poem from your colleague."

"Thanks," said Harry. "Rhyme time, over the slime of bacon and eggs, discussing the dregs…"

Mike tapped the table. "I dare not compete."

"Information?" Judge had turned serious and, therefore, a dark rubicund. He was still angry about the abortive radio transmissions.

"The victim was a six foot woman, possibly a hermaphrodite, you know, Christine Jorgeson sort, and big, strong, hairy, and having morphine in her blood." Mike frowned. "After having seen the photos, I find it hard to say 'her', don't you know?"

"'It will suffice," returned Judge.

"The killer was prepared for a big woman, or man, but that he chose to attend this rally for Ladies Freedom makes me think he targeted a Lesbian, but got two, he hoped. Speculation! We have not released any details for obvious reasons. I've got Willison and company talking to park visitors and to members of that 'group'. The crime wasn't discovered until after the meeting by a visitor who knew the couple. Someone felt the pulse of Glenda Wentworth and was smart enough to give her artificial respiration. The ambulance guys supplied oxygen, there was no heart stoppage. The garrotte wire cut her neck badly. Apparently, she's a delicate flower, but the killer underestimated the force needed."

Harry quipped, "She fainted, she feinted. One life saved."

"Ain't we clever," said Mike.

"Indeed. If she can talk, we will have a firm description of the murderer, and hopefully it will connect with the other crimes. The morphine would have been injected, I think, and this would jibe with the pimp, Amos or Andy, whoever, found with a needle in his arm. Murder after dark in the park with the trombone player. The weapons are in a countdown, don't you think? Car accident, pistol, poison, axe, lead pipe, and now, the rope."

Mike piped up, "Sure enough clues. The killer is Colonel Mustard in the Study."

"I say Mr. Green in the Conservatory."

Judge shook his head. "Enough of this nonsense. It was Professor Plum in the Kitchen…*inside a pudding…*"

Mike shook his finger, "No, it was Colonel Mustard on a hot dog…*somewhere.*"

Giselle had come and asked "Did you want to order a frankfurter?"

Harry said, "No, dear. We were speculating. Whether we should call you Miss Scarlet or Mrs. Peacock."

Before she huffed off, Giselle said "I'm a brunette, and I'm *not married.*"

That got her a big gratuity from Harry, though Judge had already paid the bill. He was cheap that way, on tipping. Harry was glad to have a new way of teasing her.

Mrs. Peacock!

Outside the restaurant, before they broke up, it was agreed that Harry and Mike would interview Glenda that afternoon in the hospital. Judge would resume his post at the golf club. They knew a physical description was forthcoming, but that its brevity, being after dark, might be trivial. What they needed was another beeper and a different channel, which meant Judge would sit with two receivers as he drank his beers. That arrangement being made, they parted.

The head nurse, Helvey Toop, "a good Latvian name," she told them, was disinclined to allow the interview. "She's still in shock."

"How would you know?" asked Mike.

Nurse Toop countered with, "Mr. Saybrook, need you wear sunglasses in my ward? The lighting has been carefully engineered."

Harry said nothing. Mike took out his badge. "This is a murder investigation, in case you didn't know."

"Of course I didn't," said the sister. "We have Ms Wentworth in on *attempted murder*. I can hardly be blamed."

"Her companion was killed, obviously," said Mike, flashing his badge in her face. "Please take us to the lady's room."

As they proceeded, Harry asked Mike, audibly, "Where do they find these people?"

Nurse Toop made a harrumphing sound and admitted them. Glenda Wentworth lay peacefully in a conglomeration of blankets and tubes. Her neck was bound, but her hands fluttered slightly. "It's the police, Ms Wentworth, for their investigation."

Mike grabbed her by the shoulder and ushered her out, then shut and locked the door. "I hope you're feeling better," he said to Glenda. "After your horrible loss."

Glenda began to weep straightforwardly, the tears flowing in even rivulets down each cheek. "My beloved Rex. I'll never see her again in this life, I know. She's gone."

"Who told you this?" Mike asked.

Glenda pointed at the door. "The nurse did. She said I ought to know."

Both men shook their heads. Harry took a small napkin off the bedside desk and gently wiped her dry. "We're very sorry, but you alone can help us find the man who did it."

He was obliged to help her blow her nose and tossed the napkin in the wastebasket, replete with its white plastic liner. "Everything will be fine."

She wanted to cry again, but murmured, "You are kind, Mister, what is your name?"

Harry told her and added, "This is Mike Herman, the homicide detective." Then he somewhat abruptly left the bed and sat in a metal chair with its sidearm of a cupholder and water glass, on empty.

Glenda looked at Mike's badge and related how she and Rex had joined the meeting. "Rex was always shy in crowds, so we saw this bench at the back and asked to sit there."

"What do you remember about the man who was there?"

"He seemed oh so nice, so kind, he seems to welcome our company. He said he supported the organization, but I thought it slightly odd that he did not sing our invocation hymn…he didn't even stand up for it."

Mike offered, "He might have been unmusical. Can you draw me a picture of him?"

"He was average height, I guess, although I only remember him seated. Rex talked with him…" she stopped and sniffled "…and they seemed to get on. When the program started there was a mosquito invasion, I mean, millions of them all at once, like a plague from Moses, and we were swishing them off, and the man handed Rex his paper to help. Then he got up and stood behind me and…"

Mike put his hand on her shoulder, "Go on."

"I felt this horrible cold thing on my neck and I felt it cutting into my skin and I thought I heard the man laughing to himself. Then I fainted."

She gave a careful description of the Man: dark, well-dressed, shaven close, and wearing some cologne she could not identify. Nonetheless, the description, as expected, was inconclusive. "Sounds like anyone," Harry said later, "but it also sounds like the mysterious guy with the custom Cadillac."

"You rest," Mike had concluded. "We'll get that bastard."

But Glenda had already fallen asleep.

"I think the loose ends are coming together," Harry remarked. They left without thanking Nurse Toop and after deliberately avoiding her.

"We don't need those types with murder victims," Mike snorted. "Jesus Christ, I wish Nurse Toop had been the fellow with the rope around her neck."

Harry grunted slightly, "You never know. She coulda done it. Or, she could be done."

"Merely an accomplice but a nice idea. It wouldn't surprise me if she helped people take the quick way out. There was case of that last year, but the 'angel of mercy' was a *male* nurse."

"Worst of all," Harry returned. "I don't think we'll be on board with the second receiver until tomorrow. Call you then."

As he got into his Ford LTD Mike smiled, relieved to have a short schedule. "Tomorrow's another day."

Harry said nothing.

26

The Man still had regrets, that the couple was totally innocent and so totally devoted. Rex and Glenda had cost society nothing. They were just fellow travellers with no bone to pick in their unnatural love nest. Yet his blood pulsed as he thought, "I've killed two love birds within five minutes. It was so easy, I was quick, and I served Death faithfully." This emotional contrast was, he knew, pathological and he loved it.

He felt, though, another pang when taking inventory. He had syringes, those were easy to get, cyanide and cocaine, but little morphine left, plus his stiletto, Bowie knife and pistol. Perhaps he should get a sawed off shotgun, or, a hunting rifle with telescopic sights. It might be hard to find, but he'd like a walking stick containing a sword. How about a modern gadget like a pen that exploded? An auto bomb, affixed to the muffler, set off by high temperature? A *letter bomb*, such as terrorists used! How about a hand grenade, and how about him, G.I. Joe, with the pin in his mouth?! Here, *catch!*

Wanting to make a new list, but already knowing it by heart and so, he took out his old one, with its last entry of a policeman, and tossed it in the trash. Had he not graduated from the cadre of shooters and assassins? He did crave a *memento mori* for each deed. A lock of hair in each case? Too morbid for words. A bit of clothing? Better. He had wanted the scalp of the trombonist. Then he thought better of the idea. The police would easily connect his efforts, if, for example, each victim had a missing thumb.

The Man had allowed himself one luxury during the last month, a silk smoking jacket, in which he liked to eat breakfast, although he rarely touched cigarettes or cigars. The latter he reserved for holiday meals. He kept an exquisite humidor of Turkish cigarettes in the living room. Tobacco had served perfectly for empty moments inside high drama, something to hold in hand and to inhale and exhale as one savored a triumph, or, when one fled a foe.

In his spate of television time he managed to watch crime shows and found a series about forensics that frightened him. With the new levels of its sophistication he was relieved he had left no culpatory trace. So it *seemed*. He had never submitted his fingerprints for a license or a job, how could that be used? There might be some minutiae from his automobile, that was a long shot too. His main worry was the emerging art of surveillance cameras, hidden away, and perhaps to focus on his face. The ones at the golf club were, he knew, more rumor than fact. They might catch Juan the chauffeur, but not "the Man"!

Another shipment coming in! He would have to plan another delivery. He saw no reason to change his *modus operandi*. Juan had told him about the examination by some lush from the Nineteenth Hole, that "Judge" and that was vaguely disconcerting. The said patron had seen him, he was sure, more than once, but who really noticed him, the Man, who was nothing without his Cadillac, a Mongol without a warhorse?

He did communicate with Juan, but it was superfluous and done in a code, through Juan's secretary. The Man was just another client. He used a name for each rung in their ladder. 'Charlie' for urgency, 'John Smith' for a pending delivery, 'Jimmy' for a prospective delay, and then, numeric codes which resembled phone numbers, but were in fact ciphers.

He considered a vacation, that was overdue! On a cruise vessel, and what greater field to harvest could there be? Nosferatu in the hold? More like, "Man overboard! Woman overboard!" Uh, uh. Not exactly. His dream murder was to have the victim torn to bits by the ship's propellor. Off the deck, through the grinder, and into the mouths of sharks! That was tasty, tasty, oh yes, tasty as the nicely-ground pre-cooked breakfast sausage on his plate.

A nap, first. Then he would make his pick up, fill the bag, leave it at the club and fulfill the expected routine. But he did need a vacation. He wanted a romance. A young floozy impressed by money, but no slut or prostitute. They could be had, at bargain prices, on those behemoth cruise liners.

Judge Rugh at first found the second receiver indistinguishable from the first, so he placed a sticky price tag from the drug store on it. Both the units seemed happy, both had a strong pulsing signal. He had checked to find the two bags, but forgot which already was bugged. The transmitter had been inserted below the golf balls, on the grounds that it was easy access but the least likely for a thorough inspection. On the second bag he put the new unit inside a small zippered slot near the bag's bottom.

The thought came, and he spoke to himself, "here are two bags, both have transmitters. If the culprit brings in the third, presumably stuffed with drugs or contraband, that will not have the beeper and the chauffeur will take it and there will be no signal. One must hope that the agent takes a bag already set to be tracked. We should, therefore, have only one signal to follow, and that would be the supplier himself, and hopefully, a man to fit the killer's profile."

Harry had reported yesterday's interview with Glenda. Then Mike had phoned Judge to ensure their new net was in place. He planned to track the bag himself in his Ford LTD, which ungainly vehicle could drive at high speeds with moderate risk. If the man in the Caddie was the perp, then Mike would have a vague idea of his car. That would allow other police cars to intercept him, should they be needed. He would love to see Bozo Willison nab the bastard, and throttle him, unintentionally, in 'self-defense'.

But it was necessary to have visual contact with whatever vehicle was "holding the bag." Enough cars had gone through the golf club parking lot to establish twenty different auto and truck types. If, for some reason, the *real* mystery man used another car, he might deny having anything to do with the big Cadillac, the most likely candidate, Judge now thought, for having killed Zelda Zlotkowski. Mike's intuition told him the man in the Caddie with the big trunk was indeed the killer *and* the purveyor of drugs. He reconsidered this view as he drove towards the Nineteenth Hole where Judge Rugh waited.

If they did apprehend the nondescript fellow Harry met, then Glenda Wentworth was their trump card. "You did not kill two people, sir, you left a witness to your felony." He might crack on that, but intuition intruded, saying "Too smart to be fooled, he'll lawyer out." Judge felt like rubbing his hands together, and raising them in prayer.

Harry was asleep at home. He had become disgusted by the complexity of the investigation and its slithering tentacles. However tempting it was to ascribe all the murders to one person, the links did not always pertain: two twilight murders in a park, two injections in the arm, two violent dissolutions, all within a month. After the initial publicity *could* come a copycat, and the case would become even more detestable. Harry preferred the 'cozy' type of crime, the housemaid who would inherit a vast estate, secretly; the closed room conundrum; the butler with the incriminating weapon, breathless, behind a secret panel.

He rolled over in his bed and willed his brain to sleep.

Before going out, the Man had spoken on the phone to a travel agent about cruises. She described the nature of such outings, the ship capacities, the endless food, the payment of final gratuities, and recommended a smaller ship populated by the elite. "You sound like a cultivated gent," she stated. "So you won't like the cattle car quality of the big liners. I'm told one now has to wait in line…at the buffets!"

"I don't want that," he said. "Price is really no object. Give me a cabin with walnut furnishings. Situate me next to a duchess."

"I can't promise *that*," she laughed. "A rich widow perhaps. Or even some rock star wanting to get away from it all." She gave details about an English company and its Norwegian competitor. "Both very posh. Very cosmopolitan too."

"Book me on that one," he said. "The English boat. I'll stop by tomorrow and pay cash."

"What name should I put on the request?"

He growled inaudibly and replied, "Just call me 'Charlie', for now."

"Please don't forget your passport, er, *Charlie*."

The delivery of cocaine or heroin by the kilogram was no more challenging to the Man than driving through a fast-food window. Indeed, he pulled into a garage that serviced his car and within several minutes received the package and inserted it into the golf bag. The mechanics there had no idea of their charge. In Boca the lawyer took care of supply details, but payments had to be in cash, picked up at the golf club, extracted and sent to him. The money often arrived in a bundle labelled "Legal Documents."

The Man and the attorney were millionaires twice over from their last two years in this network. If anyone got busted it would be Juan, who knew nothing about the lawyer and little about the Man, save for his pseudonyms.

Everyone loved these 'few moving parts.' By general understanding, if there were no more drugs in any bag, or payment for the drugs was absent, the entire deal was off, forever. How Juan conducted his retail side was of no interest to either party.

The Man decided, just before lunch, or after, and which he would take at the Nineteenth Hole, he would play nine and then fetch his bag home. The persistent idea of Señor Rugh, as Juan called him, being so curious about the golf bag, riled him and he thought to face off with the fellow, who might have seen him but could have no idea of his purposes. He therefore booked a tee time at two p.m. and planned to take his bag home as usual, empty, he thought, this time. To communicate his vacation plans to Juan, no problem. Profits would remain. Next week they would all be richer.

Mike and Judge did not get along but they made allowances. It was hopefully their last day of cooperation, and they looked forward to joining Harry for dinner, if that's how the schedule worked out. Did it not depend on circumstance?The receivers sat on their luncheon table, and both were tuned properly and emitted regular diode signals in silence, sound turned off.

The table, a huge circle that could seat six, gave Mike room for his briefcase there, which he placed on top of the receivers. Judge fussily maneuvered the dog-eared valise so he could see the flashing lights, and ordered a beer. No reason to advertise this modern technology!

"This beats a midnight stakeout in Harlem," Mike said. "You've been here for a few minutes. Anything?"

Judge shook his head. "Been thinking how hollow this case is, or could be. We have only disparate chunks of evidence. One name, from the golf bag, 'John Smith.' Bogus, and I'd be surprised if our ferret does not have many an alias."

"We don't care about that if we catch him in the act. He could plead ignorance, he took the wrong bag, that's what I would do. But let's say the light goes off and we *can* track him. I think if we find his *home*, that will open many a secret door. If necessary, I'll have the place burgled…"

"Not if you tell me about it, Mike," Judge answered. "I am a judge and there is something we call 'the law.' But to review, on the one occasion the bag took flight, shall we say, we lost the signal. However, the bag has returned, but I wasn't here to receive it, that's a simple enough deduction for now. That bag is still here, and we have the second bugged. So, if this guy comes back, he must take one of the two on the rack. And, we might hazard, *the bag he brings may contain more contraband.* Their delivery system is subtle but they may have left a history of fingerprints on the bags, let's not forget. If he is arrested for dealing in drugs, that may be a lever to force his admission to the killings. I don't feel good about this. He would have to negotiate some plea bargain, otherwise, for murder, we'll fry him in good old F-L-A."

"Here's to Sparky," said Mike, lifting his drink. "Zee olde electric chair. A condemned man ought to have a choice, like Gary Gilmore. And in my opinion, executions should be televised or made public. No matter how gruesome."

"I tend to agree, but we're getting big crowds of anti-capital-punishment types, they might overwhelm the guards and carry away the condemned. I jest. The coils of government are more tenacious when grabbing money in lieu of life. But back to the history of the last month, the quirky hit and run, the deliberate shooting, well, you have it in your head. I hope to hell the press has no idea about that lady who survived?"

"I sent our best lady cop there to 'guard' her and make sure the staff kept mum. You should be sorry you missed the head nurse, what a piece...*of work*. Glenda was still in shock, she could only chat for a few minutes. If it gets out, we may all be whistling Dixie. He's sure to bolt, and he's smart, and we'll be standing there, dicks in hand."

"I didn't see the strangling in today's paper," Judge said.

"We managed some time by charming the coroner. Mysterious death on the blotter, but he will classify it *tomorrow*." Mike ordered a sandwich, and offered to pay, but Judge refused.

"Gotta watch out for those ham sandwiches," he returned. "People have choked to death on 'em."

That almost happened to Mike. As he was swallowing a bite, Judge said, "The light has changed, look." But he rescinded the observation, he was "overwrought," which he stated in his apology. The next moment they both saw a man, medium, dark and ordinary, leave the Pro Shop with one of the bags on his cart. "That's him," said Mike, "I know it!"

However, their suspect drove the cart over to where he could park it near the restaurant. He went to a smaller table than theirs and sat down, picked up a menu, and waved to the waiter. After doing so, both men noticed that he focused on them, while trying to appear nonchalant.

"If that's our boy, he's either got big balls or has lost both of them. Crazy to come close, but he has no idea of our entrapment. Unless he's innocent." Judge called the waiter over. "I'd like to buy that man a drink," he said. "Would you invite him over here?"

Mike took off his jacket and laid it over the valise and the receivers. "Let's not tip our hand, old sport. Here he comes."

The Man sat down and introduced himself as 'John Smith.' Mike asked, "Got a middle initial?"

"Gentlemen," came the quiet voice, "we are new acquaintances. I am involved in high finance and other crimes…" he laughed theatrically "…so I use that name here. No one seems to care. I'm not all *that* frivolous. I'm sure you can find out who I am from the club roster, though I'm told its 'top secret'. This club does not admit the hoi polloi. That's one reason I joined it but you can't be in big business without belonging to some extravagant golf establishment."

Judge introduced himself and added, "This is Mike, my associate. By the way, I am a judge."

He shook both their hands firmly. "Financiers need confidentiality, as we're always accused of cheating or manipulating others. So, I confess, I am ruthless in business, but more by the book than by…hook or…by crook. As a judge, you know what I mean."

"It's rhyme time again," Mike said.

"I've seen you here before," the Man returned, "Judge Rugh, that is. Mike, I don't remember you."

"How long ago was that?" Judge asked.

"Well, I've been a member here since the club was founded, and hold one of its largest bonds, there's your clue, Judge." He chuckled. "I've been the anonymous sort for many years, never joined teams, nor clubs nor corporations, just a lone wolf. Usually play a round by myself, that's my lot."

"If I'm not mistaken," Mike asked, "don't you have a huge Cadillac, kind of rebuilt, real fancy?"

"Yes! My pride and joy. Because of my profession I need a car that can impress my clients and afford an amazing road performance. My engine was rebored and my suspension so fixed that, if I wanted to, or needed to, I can cruise at well over one hundred and twenty miles an hour."

"That's better than most police cruisers," Mike said.

"I wasn't aware of that," he answered wryly, "but don't policemen drive Fords or Mercurys around here? It's a confession, but one chased me on Highway 95 a few months ago and I was off before he could catch up. Great sport that!"

"Hope you never run into the wrong person," Mike put in. "That car would have no mercy on, let's say, a blind person at a crosswalk with his guide dog…"

Mike observed that the Man's expression did not change, but that his eyes grew smaller, almost into beads. Then he laughed shrilly. "That's a macabre thought! I drive carefully and I don't think I could live down such a tragedy. I once ran over an opossum. It just stared at me and then, I kept on driving. Those animals are stupid, but, thank you for the drink, I'm having lunch and a quick nine holes. I don't want to wolf down my lunch, as my tee time is not too far off."

"Nice to meet you, Mr. Smith," Judge said. "I'm a judge, and my business can be just as touchy as yours. Can't talk much about it. Hope to catch you again here at the club. Maybe we can shoot nine holes together, what do you say?"

The Man rose and shook both their hands. "Fine by me. I'm planning a vacation, always wanted to go on a cruise. So doggone many of them, hard to choose."

They watched him eat his lunch with moderate relish, pay cash, and get back into the cart. When he had hit his first shot, and pursued it in the cart, Judge returned Mike's jacket and moved the briefcase. "Time for the show to begin, eh wot?"

"Wonder which bag 'n' beeper he took."

Judge set the receivers neatly side by side. "We'll know in a jiffy. Did you see anything important with your policeman's eyes?"

"Yes and no. He took the collision idea with a grain of salt. The expression stayed the same, but not like a mask. That's a smart John, that Mr. Smith. His eyes almost gave him away. I thought he looked kind of…Armenian."

"He's dark but not swarthy. But Armenians come in all shapes and sizes. Like Iranians, or Lebanese. We'll find out, of course, but my guess is that his parentage is Sicilian." Judge looked at the receivers again. "It's this one," he said, touching the new one on his right. "It's beginning to flicker."

The Man's golf cart was beyond their view. The sun, on its reclining course, sent shadows over the patio tables on the Nineteenth Hole. On the third tee, the Man hit a superb shot, inches from the hole. A strong land breeze fluttered the palms that waved a tribute, their exquisite branches bent in praise.

The Man said to himself, "They may think they know something, but they don't know much. What the hell can they learn from sitting in a restaurant all day long?"

27

The coming dusk was at first a citrus orange, then blood-red, and, at last, a lemon yellow. Some chill rode bareback on the October evening wind. Mike sat next to Judge and watched the flickering on the receivers glow and grow faint, its pulses more intermittent.

"He's almost through playing, I think," Judge said. "You'd better call in your boys."

Mike had already done so, and he had walked over and noted the license plate on the Cadillac. It came back from registry as "John Smith" but with a post office box. He wondered how that came to be, they often didn't accept such addresses. He said merely, "This *would* have to happen at shift change."

Judge had returned from the boys' room, readjusted the seat cushion, then sat. "The pause that refreshes. I was going to order an early supper, you know, one can just sit here, eat and drink, watch golf, and mightily vegetate. But we'll need empty stomachs, Mr. Herman."

"There's one unmarked car near the club exit, old sport. The plate number is on the bulletin with instructions to get no nearer than a block. We should be able to see the Cadillac when it pulls out, but only if we move to the front bench. No sign of the stretch limo. Should we abscond with the other golf bag?"

"I saw Dave Chick in the clubhouse just now, he's going to put it inside the Pro Shop behind the counter. To be given to the limo driver, if asked for. That's one bird we won't have to fly over to observe. I already checked out the limo's registration and it is owned by 'Juan's Limousine Service' in a garage near the airport."

"Should I call Harry?"

Judge said "No. Give him the day off. We're going to get all the credit, Harry can bask in our glory for a change."

"He'll like that, but he should know. I'll call him when the fox begins its run. Tally ho! "

They had moved to a new perch in front of the club on the exit loop. This allowed them to see the parking lot, but in shadow. Their suspect could see them — if he looked — as he drove by. They would feign indifference and then call in the cavalry. It was pushing dark when Mike said, "There he is. Getting into his car."

The Man had come down the side path and walked cheerfully to his auto. He'd shot a record round. Judge and Mike watched carefully, and saw him store the bag inside the trunk. That was expected. They did not observe him, as he closed the lid, carefully take the magnetic license plate and reverse it, so the Georgia marker showed. It was now, to any dull traffic officer, become a different vehicle from behind.

The Man realized that the hounds had his scent, but were not really on his trail. Still, to be careful. He had noticed Judge Rugh noticing him, and he knew vaguely that Judge was important. The other man unnerved him; Mike looked too worldly to befriend a magistrate. Why had Judge Rugh approached Juan about the golf bag? If this was the bag of John Smith, why had neither man questioned him about it? He had never seen Judge Rugh playing golf, but that was happenstance. The Man guessed many of the club members could care less about golf. What other high society enclave was there in the area? He wasn't crazy for golf himself either, but one needed some sport in which to participate. Tennis was acceptable but required too much exertion, other sports were juvenile. Hemingway had said there were only three *sports*: mountain climbing, auto racing, and bull fighting, all the rest were games. The Man agreed. So he would game. He thought of Dr. Johnson's aside, "Who is ruined by gaming?"

He was playing the most dangerous of games *and* one of the oldest, the hunting, and killing of men. But the doe could prove as difficult to bag as the many-pointed buck. Life had a terrific capacity to exist. At his father's death bed he observed that, although most of his organs had failed, his father's heart kept beating, even though he could see it weakening as the veins in his face turned black. Then death came not as a spear but as a heavy stone. Death was death, the ultimate absolute!

As he drove out of the golf club circle, he noticed one auto parked by the exit that was never there before. He turned down the main road and saw two marked police cars facing each other across the street. Visceral fear tickled his spine like a venomous worm. Something was up but nothing he understood. Just drive safely and leave them in the dust!

"Get your fat ass in ASAP, Judge!" Mike had the LTD in gear and Judge was juggling the receivers and trying to open the door, which automatically locked when the car was put in gear. Mike had to unlock it, Judge entered, put the receivers on the side and fixed his seat belt. "Not as comfy as the club, eh?"

"Divine justice gives you this Ford product," his companion remarked. Judge put the secondary receiver on the floor and kept the first on the padded dash. "I'm turning on the sound," he said. "The light is beginning to show he's distancing himself. Let's go, Dick Tracy."

"The boys in blue have the plate number and a general description of the Caddie, don't worry, we'll catch up. You'll have to navigate, it's hard enough to drive safely in this crazy town."

Direction-finding was crude and simple, if Judge pointed the receiver to the right and the light dimmed, and then to the left and it brightened, they would bear left, toward the stronger signal. However, every thirty seconds or so the signal would not come. "Damn," he said, "does thing work or doesn't it?"

"There's interference with any radio wave," Mike replied. "Buildings, antennas, dips in the road, and, I should have considered this before, that custom-built could have thicker metal that attenuates the signal. Still, you *are* getting readings…"

Judge nodded. "Signal's back, we're in the right direction. If you have radio contact, check with your boys."

Mike reached down and picked up his microphone. He lifted a panel where the FM radio should have been, revealing a police two-way transmitter with a carousel of small lights and several dials. "Mike here, check in, Bozo and Gang."

"Boze here chief, we have nothing. Lots of cars but no Florida plate with JOH*SMI on it, like you tole us. One big shiny Cadillac but from out of state. We'll keep looking."

"Who's in the unmarked car?"

"Frankie here, Lieutenant. I saw a big Caddie turn south when it left the club, but it was wearing Georgia plates, like Boze said."

"I just looked at that car an hour ago and it was the Florida registry given to you guys. If you patrolmen screw this up, somebody's going to get it up the keister. Frankie, just go south and catch up with us or with the damn suspect. Big Cadillac with oversize bumpers. Just look for that! Dark metallic color, kind of coppery. Dark window tints. We're following him through a radio finder."

"OK, Lieutenant. Where are you now?" Mike told him. "Uh, we're about a half mile on your rear, we'll catch up. Want us to turn on the siren?"

"No, just put the metal down. Traffic is thin right now, do your thing and accelerate!"

"Ten-four, big ten-four."

The Man decided to play it safe, cut across to Highway 95 and speed his way north, reversing his direction. On the highway he would have four exits, and unless the State Police stopped him for speeding — but could they? —he could elude any pursuers and go home, go to a restaurant, or even a motel or hotel with a parking garage. They didn't know where he lived. If Judge and his sidekick found him, it would be inconceivable luck. Still, he felt Fear beside him like an invisible snowman. He breathed bravely and deeply. No one could beat Fate if she frowned. No one.

They could not know he had changed license plates, so he relaxed. He had done so alone in the parking lot, and in a heartbeat. The Georgia plate was of different hue and read : PEA*CHY. If the highway patrol was looking for a Florida plate, it would be white and catch their eye. If they read the Georgia plate, it would make no sense and hopefully confuse them. He was not the only Cadillac on the highway.

Traffic thickened, it grew dark more quickly, as the days were shorter. The Man felt road anger after the prick of being "discovered," and the frustration with trucks and women drivers and kids in hot rods doubled his impatience. His perfect day was dissipating. Feeling the pistol on his belt, he wanted to roll down his window and shoot any road hog in his way.

It was necessary to turn left and go through the industrial park to reach Highway 95 North. Here were numerous encumbrances: warehouses, sheds, factories, chimneys, and a huge fuel conglomerate, whose regular discharge of trucks made traffic snarl. That would slow down anybody. The area had various constrictions, the worst being narrow bridges and road construction markers. A number of tractor trailers could come out and lumber into the right lane, traffic had to halt. When things got going, people always tried to cut in and out to escape the next snafu.

The Man was again placid when he was cut off, rudely, dangerously, by a Honda Civic at high speed, driven by a young woman smoking a cigarette. She flashed it out the driver's window, and cut across his path, as if, he thought, to taunt him. Here was the most dangerous driver on the thoroughfare: the young liberated female who had learned to weave through traffic acrobatically, darting in and out, leaning on her horn or flashing her lights. "Out of my way, I'm more equal than you, Mister Driver of the oversized sedan!"

He flashed his lights and blew his horn, a custom air horn that would deafen a buffalo. "Damn you bitch!" he said, and cut her off from a turn. She rolled down her window and gave him the finger.

"So you want to die," he said and reached for his pistol. "I will oblige…" They were disparate on the highway, shooting her might work.

She accelerated but could not compete with his high performance V8 and heavy duty suspension. Screeching brakes, she flashed another insult, but lost control and tumbled, rolled, off the bridge on which they vied. Simultaneously, a huge lorry came over the hump and crashed into the Cadillac, throwing it also off the bridge. Two other cars close behind were tossed likewise aside. The truck veered right, tore the railing and went headlong into the fuel depot below.

Somehow, it exploded, shooting fire and igniting a storage tank of gasoline, used to refuel trucks supplying gas stations. The huge orange conflagration mushroomed skywards. Inside the Caddie the Man helplessly rolled in darkness, to ominous thumping, then in horrible phosphorescence, then in searing heat as his own gas tank exploded. His doors flew open in the impact, the pistol he had dropped was expelled and the trunk popped open, ejecting the golf bag into the gigantic blaze. An ocean of fire poured in upon him.

The girl had survived the crash but was thrown from her Honda into a mire of flames. Suddenly she emerged, a fiery torch that spun about the inferno, screaming and flailing her arms, until she fell to writhing on the tarmac. He screamed "Got you, you bitch!" but his lungs were already burnt dumb. The other autos, rolled into the furnace of destruction, burned, and also blew up. Before he died, the Man knew this was His Death, His funeral, and His immolation. He saw a face reflected in his windshield, a raving luminescent skull, his own visage, and then, in his mind, he glimpsed a raving hag's skeletal hand before it pulled him into Gehenna.

"Goddam," said Judge. "This effing receiver's gone off again. We were getting close. But I can't tell if he's gone south, or headed east or west."

Mike saw the glow of the fire in the distance, but thought of Halloween bonfires, not an industrial holocaust. The smoke cloud was being blown to sea by the land breeze, and what little he could make out in the darkness gave him less cheer. "We've lost him, I think, again, but we should be able to catch up...tomorrow. For Christ's sake, let's have supper, there's a barbecue down the road here, that's where we're going. Screw this crazy goose chase!"

Judge said dryly, "*You're* the driver."

Mike grunted and growled. He radioed his men and called off the chase. He didn't want excuses, he didn't want to know where they were, or where they weren't. They were assholes, and he called them that, idiots, buffoons, incompetents…but he would have to take the blame.

28

There had never been a fire like it there before. The almost complete destruction of the fuel storage tanks in the ensuing blaze, estimated at a thousand degrees, had reduced two city blocks to ashes. Inside the smoking residue lay melted autos and six humans burnt into charcoal dummies. "How in hell can we identify anyone, or anything?" asked the fire inspector.

"Put 'em in a bag, Chief, we'll figure it later," was the assistant coroner's reply. "I guess this is what fire bombings were like in the big war. Only those killed thousands. This must be like Hiroshima."

"Be careful with the human remains," shouted the Chief, "you guys, try to keep 'em intact. Holy Moses, these cars and trucks, they melted!"

A hundred yards off, a fireman said, "Hey, Joe, some free golf clubs!" He held up the driver, its shaft bent like a bow. "This could hit curve balls."

"*You're* the curve ball, Gomer!"

"Fuckin' A, man, fuckin' A!"

"Just put it in the trash bin, OK? We don't have time to shit around."

Harry insisted they go to another restaurant for breakfast, but they ended up at a donut shop with coffee and rolls, and Bozo Willison.

"What happened?" asked Mike.

"We thought we had him, there were two cars he drove by, going south, by our guesswork. You told us the direction but you lost him, the unmarked car lost you, and we proceeded until news came about the big fire, same time you called off pursuit…"

Judge said, "I'll take up my post later. A few more tries. If the fellow was that John Smith, he may be on a cruise ship, or a slow boat to China, I don't care." He tried to hold his coffee in one hand, a pastry in another. "It seems we'll have to wait on the next murder. The electronics won't fail us, I can promise you."

Mike was emphatic. "We'll arrest the chauffeur when he picks up the golf bag full of cocaine. That's certain. Then, we shake him down. At least we're breaking one link in their chain."

Harry smiled. "Have it your way, it still makes partial sense. I would assert that all the murders emanate from one person, probably that quiet man in the Cadillac. He has to show up sometime, but I'd give it a month. My money says he's off on a lark. You might check the cruise line bookings."

"At least we know what club records to check," Judge said. "But I don't think John Smith will amount to more than John Doe."

He continued to read the newspaper. "No one is sure how that fire took place. Some think terrorism, some arson, or something to do with a truck going off the road. Six people dead. Six little mummies of ash."

"Make that a list of seven dead," Mike added. "Glenda Wentworth committed suicide yesterday."

"That's tragic," said Harry.

"Hopefully the killer won't have noticed it, as the obit for Rex Booker is here too."

"Double funeral coming up," Harry noted.
"Pathetic in every sense. Innocents die in tandem. What can we say?"

Bozo Willison asked to go. "OK," said Mike. He handed five dollars to the officer. "Buy yourself and the boys a dozen."

They agreed to keep the case alive for thirty days. After that, as predicted, they would call it "a bad month." If the perp was on board some ship, what could they do? Christmas sparkled ahead on the calendar, and the New Year.

"Hopefully, a good one," said Harry.

"Agree mucho," replied Mike. "It can't be worse."

The arrest of Juan Cohones proved only that he ran a successful limousine business and that neither he, nor his secretary, knew anything about the murders. He claimed someone was trying to frame him for dealing in drugs, that it was his customer's bag, and he didn't know the customer's name. His lawyer got him off with a fine.

As for the identity of John Smith, owner of the golf bag, he said, "Who is John Smith?"

Two months later, the Man's landlord reported his tenant as missing, and offered to open the apartment, should the Police wish him to. The task fell to Bozo Willison. Missing people were a nuisance, they often showed up after their goods had been seized or appropriated. When Willison saw the luxurious penthouse, he told the landlord, "We'll look after this. Don't worry, I'll get back to you."

The landlord replied, "I'll be back. The guy who lived here dealt through his lawyer, but I don't remember the name. He just paid cash in an envelope through the office door. I might have seen him once…or twice…"

"That's all right," said Willison. "Me and the kid will search the place and report to you. We get these requests often. Sometimes it turns out people take off and leave debts, or they get married in Timbuktu and somehow return. If I find information on the lawyer it is yours."

"The Kid" was a new patrolman, Harry Peter Larsson, often teased about his name, but always called 'Pete'. Willison set him looking in the bedroom and on the balcony. Bozo went for the desk.

Inside he found the stiletto, which he adjudged to be a letter opener. There were various bills and some scribbled notes, nothing to incriminate the absent tenant. A stack of business cards, held together with a large clip, contained various merchants and one lawyer's card, which Bozo extracted. He ignored the elegant embossed card of 'Juan's Limousine Service' and replaced the the pack.

"Yeah, Pete?"

"There's nothing in the bedroom but guess what, this guy was growing Mary Jane on his porch. Like a special planter, full of *gr-rass*."

Bozo went on the balcony and inspected the secret garden. "Good work, Pete. Did you find anything in the bedroom, like, a ring of keys?"

"How did you guess? It was in a bedside table, Boze." He jangled them before Willison.

"OK, Pete. This guy's a mystery, but he's got some nice stuff. Gimme the keys. We're almost through here, go down and get the car. We shouldn't have left it parked illegal."

Willison managed to open a desk drawer with hanging files, and put the keys in his pocket with the lawyer's card. He appreciated that the lock was a Yale, and reinforced, so the drawer would have been hard to jimmy. Bozo rifled through the files, finding various deeds and stock certificates. But he knew something else might be there, and it was. A stack of fifties.

At a glance he knew he held several thousand dollars in his hand; now, it was inside his Kevlar vest. In another drawer he found the four knit golf stockings, but no other evidence about the Man. Crazy things, not worth an inventory. Bozo locked the desk. He would call the lawyer next day.

In his greed he failed to open one crucial folder, the contents of which were eventually used by the probate court as proof of identity.

It was the Man's full name, followed by Bachelor of Arts, on a sheepskin diploma, embellished by the crimson regalia of Harvard College.

THE END

Made in the USA
Middletown, DE
04 August 2020